G R JORDAN

Scrambled Eggs

A Highlands and Islands Detective Thriller

First edition

ISBN: 978-1-915562-78-4

This book was professionally typeset on Reedsy.
Find out more at reedsy.com

Eggs cannot be unscrambled

PROVERB

Contents

Foreword

The events of this book, while based around real locations around Inverness, are entirely fictional and all characters do not represent any living or deceased person. All companies are fictitious representations. No eggs were cracked in the writing of this book!

Acknowledgement

To Ken, Jean, Colin, Evelyn, John and Rosemary for your work in bringing this novel to completion, your time and effort is deeply appreciated.

Books by G R Jordan

The Highlands and Islands Detective series (Crime)

1. Water's Edge
2. The Bothy
3. The Horror Weekend
4. The Small Ferry
5. Dead at Third Man
6. The Pirate Club
7. A Personal Agenda
8. A Just Punishment
9. The Numerous Deaths of Santa Claus
10. Our Gated Community
11. The Satchel
12. Culhwch Alpha
13. Fair Market Value
14. The Coach Bomber
15. The Culling at Singing Sands
16. Where Justice Fails
17. The Cortado Club
18. Cleared to Die
19. Man Overboard!
20. Antisocial Behaviour
21. Rogues' Gallery
22. The Death of Macleod - Inferno Book 1

Kirsten Stewart Thrillers (Thriller)

Jac Moonshine Thrillers

1. Jac's Revenge
2. Jac for the People
3. Jac the Pariah

Siobhan Duffy Mysteries

1. A Giant Killing
2. Death of the Witch
3. The Bloodied Hands

The Contessa Munroe Mysteries (Cozy Mystery)

1. Corpse Reviver
2. Frostbite
3. Cobra's Fang

The Patrick Smythe Series (Crime)

1. The Disappearance of Russell Hadleigh
2. The Graves of Calgary Bay
3. The Fairy Pools Gathering

Chapter 01

The job was better in the summer. That was Joel's conclusion as he drove down the small country lane in the dark. The beam of his moderate-sized car highlighted the overhanging branches above him. The road would swing left in a minute, right at that bit where the lorries struggled to get through.

In the daylight, a certain tree looked unnaturally clipped because of the lorries gradually working away the branches at the bottom. It was a wonder the large vehicles got down the lane at all, and the owner of the egg farm, Mr Tilbury, had discussed with Joel the pros and cons of another access road.

Well, the place was enormous. He had well over sixty hectares. Thousands of birds, all arranged in barns. That was what got Joel. Free-range chickens. Yet every time he saw them, they were all shut up. That was because he came at night, of course. He'd been in the day a few times, but Joel liked the night shift.

It was quieter when you did your patrol. Security was better in the dark, better when no one was about. Joel could happily drive about with his music. He'd have his piece beside him and his thoughts to himself. It had been a couple of years now and the job had got no worse. If anything, it had got better.

Joel had taken the job because he couldn't find any other. He wasn't a security person. He remembered saying that to himself, but he'd presented well at the interview. They'd given him some training, and then he realised that, mostly, he simply drove around. Sure, he looked around places, made sure everything was okay, but then sat down through most of the night, waiting to see if the alarms were tripped. Yes, the nights when the rain was pelting down and the winds were up weren't pretty, but he was in his car for most of it. The car heater was usually blowing, which kept Joel smiling on the frosty nights.

He'd purchased a decent phone so he could set it up on the dash and watch a lot of his favourite programs. He might see the owners if he was around about eleven or twelve at night. Two, three or four in the morning? Never. Except for that other farm, the one that did the sheep. When the sheep were going into labour during lambing season, you could see the farmer, but Joel wasn't stupid. He realised this, and he was certainly looking professional when he arrived on that farm. The others, he met the owners so infrequently, he could wing the odd early morning meeting.

The road ahead did indeed swing left, then swung hard right before the branches eventually cleared. Joel saw the sign sweep past him. 'Tilbury's farm, eggs-xactly what you need.' It was a shocking pun, but it was for the eggs that Tilbury sold himself. They had a few rare breeds up by the house, eggs that weren't going to the mass market. Tilbury sold these, and he told Joel that he made little from them. It was more his wife's thing. Something she enjoyed.

He'd taken Joel out to the barns, though. *It's quite a sight,* Joel thought, that first time when he opened the door, and he saw all those chickens. The noise was incredible, but he was also shown the holes for access in and out.

'Eight hours a day of freedom,' Tilbury had said, which in winter was basically the daytime. In summer, they got out for longer, but not through the night. Even though this far north, the light never truly went in the middle of summer, the hens were still shut in for part of the night.

Tilbury was very proud of his operation. When he had marched Joel through the barns, showing the feeding stations, and where the hens roosted, he said it all with a tremendous sense of pride. Joel, however, had been walking along trying to make sure he didn't put his feet in any chicken shit because that's what he saw a lot of. He wondered what it would be like working there. Every day, sweeping it, pushing that chicken poo out of the way.

Joel parked up down a small lane that was close to Tilbury's large barns. He stared at one from the outside. It was an elaborate construction in some ways. A big shed, but it looked so modern. There were signs posted here, there, and everywhere. On the outside, there were security lights that would light up as soon as Joel moved towards them. Joel liked that about them. In other places he visited, he had to take the torch out with him when patrolling.

When first considering the job, Joel had wondered what would happen if he ever got attacked. The security firm had told him from the start that most of the time, he would interrupt someone who would run. If indeed, he ever interrupted anyone at all. Most places were safe, and if he interrupted someone who was dangerous, he'd phone the police. He was a security guard. He wasn't a have-a-go hero. Well, Joel didn't

3

need to be told that.

Joel stepped out of the car, opened the rear door and put on his large jacket, pulling a beanie hat down around his ears. Next, a large pair of gloves came on, and Joel made sure he had his pocket torch with him. His phone was in his jacket, and he shivered slightly with the cold air. It wouldn't be that long, a month or two, and the temperature would rise significantly, but right now, the middle of the night was cold.

Before he started his patrol, he opened the front door again, reached inside for the thermal coffee cup, and drained a little more liquid from it. He replaced it in the holder, shut the door and strode up to the barns. He would sweep around them all before he was done.

Walking along the small gravel path, Joel got close to the first barn and the security lights sprung on. He looked left and right, saw no one, and walked around the perimeter. The barn was shut up tight, with all the access holes for the hens closed over, and he made his way over to the next one. Once again, the security light came on. Joel looked around and then stopped. He could hear something. In fact, he could hear quite a bit.

In the dead of night, hens were quiet. Very quiet. The interior would be dark. The hens would sleep, all perched, some of them huddled together, awaiting the morning, or the lights flicking on inside the barn. Then their busy life of feeding, scratching away at the ground, taking a wander outside, pooing—which seemed to take up most of their day—and laying an egg, would begin. Right now, they rested all together, all silent. Or at least they should be.

It began, Joel thought, at the far end of the barn. There was some squawking. Joel walked to look around the rear, but the door was shut. There was nothing untoward looking. He took out his torch and shone it outside the perimeter of lights from the barn security system. He could see nothing further out, except the other barns. There wasn't any noise coming from them, but the noise inside the barn was building. There was a loud clucking.

Chickens were funny—Tilbury had told him—all individuals, all their own personalities. Yes, they were like a load of bickering old women when they started talking. They would shout and they would have a go at each other. One hen at the top of the pecking order would peck another at the bottom, putting them back in their place. They would walk off a bit and complain, and then the next one would kick off.

Tilbury had rattled on and on about them, but Joel imagined that this would be something when you had maybe eight or ten chickens. But there were hundreds in the barn. The barn was almost like a nightclub at closing time. Joel had been there, hearing the excited rush, the drunken comments to people, yelling for taxis, working out where they were going. Sudden silence when the music dropped, filled by a cacophony of human chickens.

He wondered what was bothering the feathered variety. For a moment, he thought maybe he should go inside, but they were chickens. They could get spooked by anything, couldn't they?

They'll soon settle down, thought Joel. *I'll just stand around for a bit.* He went to walk away over to the next barn, but the rising tsunami of cawing and cackling didn't stop. Joel turned back and thought he could hear something inside. Was he observing something?

He spotted orange at the rear of the barn and lots of smoke,

smoke pouring out. Joel turned to run and take himself away from the barn because he wasn't going inside to rescue any chickens. The whole rear of the barn was suddenly aflame. He grabbed his phone, dialling 999, standing at what he thought was a safe distance, gradually moving back towards the first barn.

'Which service do you require?'

'Fire,' said Joel. He hung on the phone, watching the fire build, flames licking out the side of the building, and up through the roof.

He heard the operator on the far end announce himself and ask what the emergency was.

'I'm at Tilbury Egg Farms, just outside of Inverness. We have a fire inside one of the barns. It's full of chickens.' Joel suddenly realised something else. The acrid smoke was in the air.

'Are you safe, sir?' asked the voice on the other end.

Joel turned and saw that the first barn he'd investigated was now also ablaze.

'I thought so,' said Joel, running back towards the car. 'I thought so.'

'Help! Help me!' came a shout. *It's from that second barn,* thought Joel. He turned to look back, but the flames were licking around the outside.

'My God, there's someone inside. It's not just chickens. There's someone inside,' said Joel.

'We're dispatching units,' said the voice on the other end. 'Don't take any risks. Don't go in yourself. Is there anything you can attack the fire with?'

'It's too big for that. Way too big. It's ablaze,' said Joel. 'It's completely ablaze. There's someone inside, there's—'

Joel looked over at the other chicken barns. They were all going up. All of them. The entire farm. Joel turned, running back to his car. As he reached it, he looked back, and the smoke pummelled towards him on the wind. He choked.

'Are you safe, sir? Are you in a safe place?'

'I'm stood away from them. There are barns, twenty of them, at least, all gone up.'

'You said there was someone inside? Are you sure of that?'

'I heard a cry for help,' said Joel. 'Somebody was shouting. They were yelling.'

'Can you hear them now?'

'No,' said Joel, 'I'm too far away. There's—' A chill ran down Joel's spine. Someone was inside. Was that what started the chickens? Was somebody trying to get out? It wouldn't be that difficult to get out from the inside, would it? Surely not.

Joel stood, watching the orange flames. The entire farm was now alive with the cries of panicked chickens, the sounds reverberating, echoing in Joel's head. It was one of the most horrific things he'd ever heard, but he tried to steal himself. They were only chickens. But he'd heard that voice, too, that voice crying out.

Mesmerised by the fires, Joel eventually caught the sound of the fire engines arriving. He turned and ran over, pointing at the fire, but in truth, it was pretty obvious what was happening. A man with a white fire hat on came towards him, asking was anyone in there, pointing at the burning barns.

'Yes,' said Joel, 'I told the man on the phone. There was someone inside. The second barn. There was somebody in that second barn.'

'Are you sure?' the man asked.

'Yes.'

7

'What about the others?'

'There shouldn't be anyone. They're chickens. It's the chickens we can hear.' Sides of barns fell down and suddenly chickens were running everywhere.

'Second barn,' said the fire officer.

'Yes,' said Joel, 'I don't think there's anyone in any of the others. I can't be sure, but there shouldn't be. There shouldn't be anybody in that one!'

Joel was helped further back from the blaze and stood to watch as the fire crews went to work. They ran lines of hoses, the initial bursts coming from the fire engines' tanks, water being poured onto the blaze. The smell of burnt chickens was everywhere, and he wondered how long before Tilbury would make his way over. Their house was a little way away, but he couldn't miss this horror.

Joel sat on the bonnet of the car, the cloy smell of smoke fumes and burnt chicken flesh making him feel sick. Several firemen asked him at different times 'Was he okay?' and he nodded. An ambulance arrived, and they ran to him to check he was okay, but Joel was staring at the second barn. The firefighters were being beaten back repeatedly.

It was over an hour and a half before they could gain access. By then, the uniformed police had arrived. Joel was questioned about what was going on, and the Tilburys were there. There were tears in the old man's eyes and Joel wondered what it must be like to see your livelihood, to see everything you've worked for, what you've built over those many years, suddenly going up in smoke. Then Joel didn't care.

He just wanted away, wanted out of security. He wanted to do some boring nine-to-five desk job because the scene before him was frankly too much. Tears streamed down his own eyes.

The barns were still ablaze, albeit not as strong as they were before. Loose chickens were running away and hiding, and the cries of Tilbury and his wife echoed in his ears.

All his senses were being assaulted, but the one that rang the hardest was the echo of the cry for help—the man inside the chicken shed. If Joel had only gone and looked, could he have prevented this? When the chickens had kicked off, if he'd gone in, would he have saved him? Joel hung his head. He would never know.

Chapter 02

An arm snaked across Hope's midriff and then pulled her in tight. She could feel John's chest touching her back. It was warm, much warmer than her, but she'd got used to that. Hope would have blankets over the bed to keep her warm. Although she'd resisted an electric blanket, saying she wasn't that old, sometimes she'd thought about it.

Their relationship had begun with them sleeping with nothing on. Now she would be more wrapped up, a pair of pyjamas, some sort of nightwear on, often bed socks too. Hope had worried about this. Was this the magic going out of the relationship? John had told her he would remove the bed socks if he felt that way inclined.

Their relationship was moving to a different place. She knew that. Not that she was annoyed with this. There was security in John. Maybe not the same initial excitement, although they still very much had their moments. There was no lack of hunger for her from him, or him from her. It was just that moments now were less frantic, more loving. Was that the word?

She wriggled backwards, letting him envelop her completely. As a woman who was six feet tall, no man was ever going to tower over Hope. She felt John was more capable of doing this when he cuddled her in. Everyone saw her as that strong, determined female figure. With John, she became someone else. Hope found herself because she had nothing to fear.

'I think it's going to be a cold one outside,' said John. 'At least I'll get to stay in the office most of the day.'

'The joys of being in charge,' said Hope. 'We've been pretty quiet too. At least I won't have to be outside, organising a cordon or a house search. When Seoras was away, it was good, too. I felt like I had the office to myself. Felt like—'

'Shall we stop talking about work?' asked John. 'Why don't we talk about something else?'

'What else would you like to talk about?' teased Hope. She knew fine, rightly. She felt his hand move down and touch her belly.

'We both want one, don't we?' said John.

'Of course,' said Hope. 'I just didn't know when the correct time was.'

'There is no correct time, is there? If we wait, you'll say you need to get settled in your role as an inspector. Then you'll need to get a few more years behind you. You'll be too busy because you're called away on this or that. Then you'll be looking to be a DCI.'

'DCI?' laughed Hope. 'I won't be able to have children by the time I'm a DCI.'

'Why?' asked John, his other hand ruffling her red hair. 'You're smart. You're clever. Macleod will not be there forever. You know that, don't you?'

'Some people have told me I should move back down to Glasgow. Move to Edinburgh. Move somewhere else. Different murder team. Rack up the experience. I could go

11

really high.'

'Well, I could probably transfer,' offered John.

'I don't want to,' said Hope. 'I like it here. The Highlands have become home. If I am going to have a little kid—'

'Kids,' said John.

Hope slapped him on the thigh. 'Kids,' she said. 'I want to be here. I don't want to be in the city.'

'Good,' said John. 'Me neither.' He kissed her on the side of the cheek. 'Is it time we made a start, then?'

'Completely,' said Hope. She turned her head to one side, allowing him to kiss her. His hands were no longer on her belly.

Hope's mobile phone vibrated.

'Just leave it,' said John. 'It'll just be some stupid message.'

The phone kept vibrating. It wasn't a message. Somebody was calling.

'Bollocks,' said Hope. 'Bugger, bugger, bugger.' John's hands released. Hope rolled across the bed, picking up her phone. It had Ross's name on it.

'Alan. This had better be important. Because if it's not, my good man is coming over to see you.'

'Sorry,' said Ross. He paused for a moment as if taking in the information that Hope had given. 'Really sorry,' he said, 'because you're going to have to come out for this one.'

'What's up?'

'Tilbury's egg farm. The big one outside Inverness. All ablaze. Except we got somebody inside.'

'What, an accidental death? You can cover that, Alan. You don't need me for that. Just have a look, get the report, and—'

'No, sorry, Hope. The thing is, the security guard was out here. He heard someone inside. The fire people said that, possibly, this is an intentional fire. Lots and lots of different barns, all gone up. Possibly incendiaries. We may be looking at a deliberate killing.'

'Okay,' said Hope. 'I'm on my way.'

Hope closed the call, turned over and looked at John.

'I'm so sorry,' she said. 'It looks like a killing. A proper one.'

'I could be quick.'

'No,' said Hope. 'I want it to be memorable.'

'Isn't it always?' said John, laughing.

Hope flung the bedclothes back, rolled out of bed, suddenly aware that the bedroom was somewhat colder than underneath the duvet. She flung her pyjama top off, followed by the bottoms. Stepping across the room, she pulled open a drawer to find some underwear.

'That's just unfair,' said John. Hope turned round. 'That's positively not on.'

'Think about cars or something,' she laughed.

Two minutes later, Hope was changed, her red hair tied up behind her head in a ponytail. John had jumped out of bed once he'd seen her start to change. By the time she was leaving the front door, he was handing her a cup of instant coffee.

'I'm not getting out of it,' she told him. 'It's time. It really is time.'

He'd stayed at the door watching her as the car departed, and Hope was thankful for the image she had. She was no doubt about to walk into something horrible. The more she got into this job, the more it went on, she realised that the good things had to be soaked up like a sponge. Your barrier of protection, your realisation that life was genuinely pretty good. Normal things were happy times.

Tilbury's egg farm was approximately three miles outside

of Inverness, occupying many acres. It had a winding road with trees providing a natural roof to the road. Approaching the farm, Hope could see the police cars and the cordon at the end of the road, stopping anyone from getting to the farm. A young officer stepped out, observed Hope through her car window, and waved her on.

She had grabbed a T-shirt, and threw it on with her jeans and her leather jacket. She had taken to wearing something a little more formal when she was in the office. But when she went out, Hope had decided that she would be her. Macleod had raised an eyebrow, the first time she'd worn a skirt with the jacket and blouse. He'd asked her why and she'd told him he'd always worn his suit. He'd said he hadn't changed, why had she? It wasn't his fault he'd grown up in a time when a shirt and tie were everything. He just couldn't get away from it now.

Maybe it was confidence. She had the inspector's job. She knew what she was doing. All her time in the force, there was always that moment of doubt with her. That hesitation she carried. Macleod had worried about it.

She knew that, but he had stepped aside, or rather stepped up. She knew he had wanted to just sit on the inspector role. DCI was not where he really wanted to be. He was up there for her. She was sure of it. He'd moved away. He might ask to move back down or maybe he would just retire. Seoras couldn't have that many more years left, could he? He was a good boss, though. If she was going off on maternity, he would handle it.

Maternity. She laughed at herself as she scanned the farm in front of her. There was smoke rising from many barns, and she could see the mobile forensic unit already there. There were fire engines too. She reached inside the car and pulled on a tabard that said 'POLICE.' There was a lot of moving about today. It'd be better if she were easily identifiable. Ross would have the scene covered for police, but it stopped everybody marching forward and pulling you back every two minutes.

She looked over towards the third barn along. Hope saw a familiar figure marching towards her. He wore suit trousers and jacket with tie, but with a much younger look than Macleod ever did.

'Boss,' he said.

'Hope,' said Hope back to him. 'Talk to me, Alan.'

'Sorry about—'

'It's fine,' she said. 'Talk to me.'

'Security guard Joel Hagberry comes up on his normal routine rounds; says he went up by the barns. Second one he went to, said he heard the chickens inside being greatly disturbed. A lot of agitation, but he didn't go in. Normally, Hagberry comes up and goes around all the barns, just checking nobody's about. He said that the outside lights all came on as they should do. They're on those infrared settings.'

'The chickens were disturbed. Did he not go in to investigate?'

'He said no. He said anything can agitate the chickens, so he thought it best just to go along, do the rest of the barns, then he would come back and see how they were then. Except he didn't get very far. Fire broke out in each and every one of the barns. He said he heard a cry inside for help, a male voice. He tried to get in, but couldn't. Called the fire brigade and ourselves. By the time the fire service got here, according to the fire chief, whoever it was inside was gone. We've got the fire investigation officer up with Jona, seeing what they can tell. It took them a while to put these fires down. They're still hot and I'm not sure you can walk in yet. Forensics are being careful. Initial findings, though, are saying deliberate fires at several sites.'

'If someone was inside,' asked Hope, 'why didn't they just get out? Or is the chicken barn locked?'

'Yes, except that you can get out from the inside. There's an electronic door locked to the outside, which can be overridden with an electronic tag.'

'Are they recorded?'

'No. Very basic system. No logging,' said Ross.

'We're thinking that whoever's inside is what? Either been half drugged, or that they can't find their way out. Been tied up, struggled?'

'We do not know how long they were alive for. Were they secured? We don't know,' said Ross. 'It seems strange they couldn't get out. The interior would've been in darkness, I believe, with a load of chickens around you, but you'd find your way to the wall, surely. Then when the fire starts, you'd be able to see. I'm thinking he must have been secured. We'll have to see what Jona and the fire investigation officer say. That could be a while though. You know how these things work.'

'Where's the rest of the team?'

'Rest of the team?' queried Ross. 'We've only got Cunning-ham left. Unless there was a priceless painting in the middle of that barn, I don't think Clarissa is going to join us.'

Hope laughed. 'No, you just get used to it. I take it the big boss hasn't appeared.'

'No, I thought you should ring him, not me. I know you need to be informed, but he doesn't need to be out for this. It's a suspicious death, but it will not be public headlines.'

'No, but I'm wondering what effect on egg production this is all going to have.'

'I've had a thought about who's inside though,' said Ross. 'Cunningham went up to the owners of the farm, the Tilburys. They're up at the farmhouse. It's about a mile to walk. They can't find their son, Roy Tilbury. I think it's him inside. Too many things line up,' said Ross. 'Jona says she'll be doing her best to try to match the body up.'

'If there's much left inside to do that.'

'Still waiting,' said Ross. 'Got units out asking for witnesses on the nearby farms. Put a stop on the road to see if anybody was driving past. Putting it out on the local news to see if anybody saw anything.'

'Good. Are you going to need anybody assisting, uniform?'

'Not at the moment,' said Ross. 'Uniform's out here with us. I don't know what I'm having to check yet.'

'I'm going to head up to the farmhouse,' said Hope. 'Keep me posted if anything develops, Alan.'

'Okay,' said Ross. 'I am sorry to pull you away from—'

He stopped. Hope blushed.

'I shouldn't have dumped that on you,' said Hope. 'It's okay. I think there may be other times.'

She tried not to grin as she walked back to the car. Someone was dead, and this could be the worst part of it, having to tell a parent their son wasn't coming home.

Chapter 03

H ope approached the farmhouse, leaving her car in the drive. The officer on the door of the house recognised her and stepped aside, but Hope stopped for a moment.

'Who have we got inside with him?'

'One of your own, Susan Cunningham, I believe,' said the officer, 'and two of ours.'

'Can you go inside and get Susan out for me, please? I want to talk to her before I talk to the family.'

Hope could hear wailing from inside the house. The uniformed officer nodded before disappearing inside. A minute later, Susan Cunningham stepped out, looking bleary-eyed.

'How long have you been here?' asked Hope.

'Got the initial call. I was on call last night. Came out; Alan followed, not long after.'

'How is it in there?'

'What do you expect?' asked Susan. 'Absolute mess. Mother's been in tears for hours. They were woken up by the commotion. Next thing, he's out running around after his chickens trying to contain them.'

'I guess there would have been—'

'Chaos is the best way to describe it. The animals were terrified, running under trees, hiding here, there, and wherever. That's the ones that haven't been cooked. Absolute carnage out there. I'm sure you smelt it as you arrived.'

'The owner's going to have a lot on his hands then.'

'I daren't look at the mother,' said Susan. 'I came up here once Ross was on the scene. Dragged the father back. Then they realised Roy wasn't about.'

'That's the son.'

'Yes, Roy Tilbury.'

'What is he, a teenager?'

'Oh, no. No, no, Roy's heading towards forty. The older Tilbury, his father, he's heading for retirement, as is the mother.'

'What, the son still lives here?'

'Yes. No girlfriend, no partner or wife. I don't know if that's by choice, if he's a playboy, or if he's just somebody under mother's apron strings. Either way, he has got no one as far as we can make out.'

'Where was he then and why are you convinced he's in there?'

'I'm not convinced he's in there, but he's certainly a possibility. Ross had one of those feelings. Thing was, Roy went out last night. Off to the Drowsy Duck, one of the pubs near here. Apparently, a lot of the egg farm community go there.'

'The egg farm community? You're telling me there's an egg farm community?' queried Hope.

'Yes, I guess it's like a gang of farmers. They all work similar hours, so they all turn up at the same place. Going back, I believe there was a lot of kindred spirit amongst them. I'm not sure how much it holds these days, but they visit the same

19

places. I mean, we do, don't we? Police officers—we've got our pubs.'

'I suppose so,' said Hope. 'Anyway, he's gone down there last night?'

'Yes. Haven't been there yet, something we must do, but we got on to the phone company about his mobile. The parents said that he'd returned to the house about ten o'clock.'

'Did they see him?' asked Hope.

'Possibly heard him go into his room.'

'What did the phone company say?'

'His phone was pinged on a nearby mast, so in a general sense, yes, he was in the area. The radius could be fifteen, twenty miles, but it is in this direction. The arc, the cone that they're talking about, puts him potentially within the farm property so that tallies.'

'Any reason anybody would want to kill him so far?'

'Roy Tilbury was due to take over this business next year. It's worth a large amount of money. This is possibly the biggest farm for eggs in the area. There's going to be a serious problem with egg production. It's mad the number of chickens they have here. You won't believe it, Hope. You really won't.'

'Why? How much are we talking about?'

'The thing is, Donald Tilbury, the father, has been talking. Mother's been crying her eyes out, but he's been talking away. He said to me that the industry in the UK has about almost forty million chickens. He said that in terms of production, there were 10.5 billion eggs produced. Most of them, ninety percent plus, from here in the UK. He said at most normal holdings, you're going to get at least sixteen thousand chickens, but theirs was much bigger.'

'Did we have anybody sorting the surviving chickens?' asked

Hope.

'The trouble is, they're a business asset. Donald's got two things on the go. He's panicking about Roy, but he's also panicking about these chickens. He's cares for them in a farming way.'

'I guess I better talk to them. Is the mother okay to speak to?'

'Had to call the doctor out to her. I believe she's lying down at the moment. Although she was wailing. He's trying to get her to sleep, or at least relax a little. She's not in a good way.'

'Let's talk to his father, then.'

Hope went to step inside, but Cunningham put her hand up, walked in and then came out with a man who was dressed in a boiler suit.

'Mr Tilbury, this is DCI Hope McGrath.'

'I'm sorry for the destruction on your property. You lost your hens,' said Hope. 'I understand your son's missing as well. We'll work as fast as we can to locate him.'

Hope stared at the man's face, which just looked shocked. The morning light was up, and looking back towards where Hope had arrived on the farm, little trails of black smoke were still rising into the air.

'It's all gone,' he said. 'All gone, thousands of them. The rest are everywhere at the moment. There's some at the back of the house. We need to find them. We need to bring them back, and I've got nowhere to put them. You can't just—'

'I appreciate the chickens are your business—' started Hope.

'They're out there, scared. They need to come back in. We need somewhere to home them. A temporary shelter set up, somehow.'

'We need to find your son,' said Hope. 'DC Cunningham

21

here says that he was down at the Drowsy Duck pub.'

'Yes, he always goes down there. It's where we meet, especially the younger ones. I don't go as much as I used to, but for generations, we've always used the Drowsy Duck. It's an egg pub.'

'An egg pub?'

'When you go about, you have your pubs you go to. Here, it's where we have meetings. We've got a little society where we come and talk about the business and that for the local area, not for the national area, set up a long time ago. Of course, eggs were sold much more locally than before all the supermarkets, all free range though. I've always been free range. Free range is the best. Free range was the norm. Then they had the cage birds for years. Now back to free range; everybody has to be free range again. All these marks and then supermarkets wanting you to do this, do that. They don't leave it up to the egg farmers, do they? We know best. They're our chickens, our hens to look after.'

The man was rabbiting on.

'Who has access to your barns?' asked Hope.

'We've got several farm hands. It's easy to get in. They're designed to keep foxes out, animals, keep the hens in safe. During the daytime they can come out, wander around. There are plenty of people about. We've got fencing and that, but at nighttime, foxes are clever. You wouldn't see them, and if they got into one of those places, they'd go wild, spook the chickens as well. When a chicken gets spooked, sometimes they just, well, they go.

'You could get hold of one of our keycards to open any of the barns. We store a lot of them in the farmhouse buildings. They're not locked away. Nobody comes in to steal your chickens or your eggs during the night. It's not what people do.'

'Yet, you have a security guard who comes around.'

'That's recent.'

'In what way?' asked Hope.

'We've had a few issues.'

'Have you? Tell me more.'

'Not just us, several of the farmers around here. We've been having a bit of argy-bargy. People are thinking other people have done it. The egg community at the moment is a bit fractured because of the changes coming up.'

'What changes?' asked Cunningham.

The man walked forward from the front of the house, forcing Hope and Cunningham to follow him. As he walked down the driveway, he stopped and turned. 'All this is going to be Roy's. Roy is going to own it all. The thing is, as big as it is, everything's getting bigger. You want to make money with the supermarkets, you need to be big in supplying them. Roy knows this. He understands business. Roy's going to take over all the eggs. Different day for me; that's why Roy's taking the business on. Clever. Roy's always clever, growing the business, you know.'

'You said you used to all meet. You still do that?' asked Hope.

'Yes, I chair those meetings, but it's not like the old days. Nowadays it's for the annual events. We've had some get-togethers. Back in the day, it would have been a dance or a barbecue picnic; different people would host; local industry get together. Like I said, it's more national now. You don't sell to the same people as we used to.

'This was my farm. This is where I grew the business. Took it from small starts, back when free range wasn't popular.'

The man suddenly sat down on his driveway, his head falling forward, tears streaming from his eyes.

'This is for Roy,' he said. 'All for Roy. Roy's going to have this. Where is he? Where is he? He went to the pub. You tell me where he is.'

'We're going to do our best to find him,' said Hope. She stepped over to Cunningham, tapped her on the shoulder, and pulled her to one side. 'Get him into the doctor, too. We'll come back and talk to him a bit more in a moment. I want to get down to that pub, see if anything happened down there that can give us any more detail.'

'It seems like he may have come back,' said Cunningham, 'or certainly it looks like his phone did.'

'He's not been positively identified returning, so we want to see how he left the pub and when he left the pub. I get the impression from his father that things are changing. We're going to need to understand the area and about the people, but the pub's a good place to start. Take him back inside and we'll get a handle on what's going on. If this pub is the centre for where they all meet, maybe the landlord knows about them all, might give us a perspective away from the actual farms themselves.'

Cunningham stepped forward and helped Donald Tilbury up from his feet, urging him back inside the house.

Hope took out her mobile, placing a call to Ross. 'I've just been talking to Donald Tilbury, Roy's father. He's in a bad way. He says his chickens are going to be everywhere. Talk to the uniform sergeant. There's going to have to be some sort of SSPCA or industry involvement in all of this. You're going to have chickens everywhere.'

'I'll get on to that; don't worry,' said Ross. 'Have you got any

24

idea if it is Roy in there?'

'I'm with you. The hunch is, it is Roy. Until Jona confirms, we won't know that. I'm going down to the Drowsy Duck, apparently where he came from. According to Donald Tilbury, that's where the egg families in the area have met for years. I want to see if the landlord is someone who's been there for a while, to get the low-down on the farmers. If Roy has been killed, and for a good reason, he might know.

'Apparently, Roy was going to take over the business next year. Roy grew it. Roy has been instrumental in developing it. Donald was banging on about the supermarkets and having to be big for the supermarkets. I think we're going to have to learn a lot about the egg industry.'

'About 10.5 billion eggs are eaten every year by the public in this country; by that, I mean the UK, obviously,' said Ross.

'How do you know that? That's what Donald said. Did you talk to him?'

'Just read it somewhere,' said Ross.

He isn't just good at computers, is he? said Hope. *That brain of his is a computer in its own right.*

'I'm off to the pub,' said Hope. 'I'll call you once we're done there. We'll need to regroup. With everything that's going on, I want another constable on this, though,' she said.

'I'm sure I can handle it.'

'Alan, I appreciate this is the first case with you as the DS, but you need help. Uniform's going to have fun and games as well. I'll give Seoras a kick, get somebody else in. We could do with someone, anyway, in the future. We've always run with DCI, DS, and at least two DCs, or at least a DS covering DC.'

'Okay, if that's what you want.'

'It is what I want,' said Hope. 'I'll speak to you soon.' She closed down the call and immediately rang John's mobile.

'I hope you've got out of bed by now.'

'I'm on my way to work,' John said.

'Bad news,' said Hope. 'This looks like a proper case. I don't know when I'll get home.' There was a deep sigh on the other end of the phone. 'I am serious about this,' said Hope. 'It's time.'

'Okay,' said John, but his voice said he wasn't believing her.

'I've got to go,' said Hope. 'I love you to bits, mister.'

There was a 'love you' response, but she knew he was disappointed. She suddenly had a bad thought. *Macleod had never had kids. Clarissa didn't have kids. Ross had a kid, though, but then again, he didn't have to make one.*

'You ready?' Hope looked for the sender of the shout. 'Your car or mine?' said Cunningham.

Chapter 04

While Cunningham drove Hope's car down to the Drowsy Duck, Hope called Macleod to update him on what was happening. He would have made the office by now, and if she didn't report in, she'd be getting a call anyway asking what was happening. He'd be champing at the bit, wanting to know if he was required.

That was the trouble with Seoras being the DCI. The smaller cases which she could handle on her own and didn't require him still meant he was itching to get involved. A desk and paperwork weren't Macleod. He was a detective. Detecting was what he did. He missed the people, missed seeing them face to face. Seoras was one of those detectives who could feel what was happening long before he proved it. It didn't remove the burden of proof but he read people better than anyone she'd ever known.

'A very good morning to you,' said Macleod.

He's itching for something, thought Hope. *Itching to be involved.*

'Morning,' said Hope. 'I'm just in between speaking to people, so I thought I should update you.'

'Here I am, ready to be updated. Tilbury Egg Farm, I take it.'

Why am I bothering? thought Hope. He'll know everything

by now, having phoned down to the desk sergeant. He'll have put feelers out to everyone in the station, stopping them as he walked along if he thought they knew anything. Probably grabbed the night shift coming off duty.

'We've been up at Tilbury Egg Farm. It's pretty decimated. Not the farmhouse or some of the other facilities, but the barns where the hens are kept. Ross has got his hands full at the moment, Seoras. Chickens everywhere. I've got a fire investigation unit there trying to work out exactly what happened. Jona's with them and we've got a potential missing person who may have been in one of the barns.'

'Murder?' asked Macleod.

'Not determined yet, but certainly a strong possibility.'

'Do you need me to come down, give you a hand?'

'No,' said Hope, rather more firmly than she'd expected.

'Oh,' said Macleod. 'Got it all under control because there'll be serious press with this? That's something you need to understand. Egg production is pretty big. Apparently, 10.5 billion eggs produced a year.'

'Have you been talking to Ross?' asked Hope.

'No. Eggs are big business and everybody has eggs, don't they? You always see it on the shelves in the supermarket,' said Macleod. 'All the eggs and they're gone that day and then the next batch comes in. Tilbury's is one of the biggest.'

'You've looked that up,' said Hope.

'What I'm saying is, this could be quite a big public case once they realise somebody's been killed in it. It also will affect the egg production, so that's going to highlight it, anyway. People will talk about it in the supermarkets if the shelves don't have eggs there.'

'I don't need you on this case,' said Hope. 'You're the DCI. It's a single murder if it is indeed murder. We're in our preliminary investigations. What I could do with is another constable. A detective constable.'

'I could pop down and do that.'

'No,' said Hope. 'It was one thing the other time when we didn't have someone and you were coming down to give me a hand like a sergeant. I don't need a sergeant. I need a detective constable and that will not be you because Ross will never give you orders or instructions.'

'No, fair enough,' said Macleod. 'Unless it's got something to do with a laptop.'

'Everybody can give you instructions on the laptop,' said Hope. She heard a laugh beside her and gave a piercing glare at Cunningham. She suddenly went tight-lipped.

'Did somebody in that car laugh at that?' asked Macleod.

'Of course not,' said Hope.

'You're not driving, so it must be Cunningham. You know you should start giving her some scenes to handle. Get Ross to go about with you.'

'I'll run this team the way I want to. I don't have to do it the way you did it.'

'No,' said Macleod, 'but I managed. I think I did okay, didn't I?'

'Enough,' said Hope, realising he was prodding her now. 'I'm off to the local pub, the Drowsy Duck. Our man, Roy Tilbury, who's missing, presumed to be the body that's inside one of the barns, was there last night. It's also the primary hub of egg-farm drinking, as far as we can gather.'

'Go gently. The landlord will be asleep, probably.'

'You never go gently. When do you ever march gently into anywhere?'

29

'You just said you would not operate like me,' said Macleod.

'Later,' said Hope. 'I'll speak to you later. Don't pester Ross.'

'I'll keep out of your way,' said Macleod. 'I'm meeting with Clarissa anyway this morning. She's educating me in eighteenth-century paintings.'

'Enjoy,' said Hope, closing down the call as Cunningham pulled up in front of the Drowsy Duck. Approaching the front door, Hope gently tapped on it, looking around for a bell, and then she hit it harder. Eventually, a window opened up above.

'The pub's shut. What pub opens at this hour?'

'Apologies,' said Hope, looking up and pulling out her warrant card. 'I'm Detective Inspector Hope McGrath. This is Detective Constable Susan Cunningham. Do you mind if we come in?'

'Keep it quiet,' said the man, looking down at them. He was clearly still in a pyjama top, and he looked behind him, into what presumably was his bedroom. 'I don't think the missus is up yet. Wait there, I'll be down in a moment.'

Hope gave him a nod and stood calmly in front of the door.

'Should we bring the missus down as well, in case she saw something last night?' asked Cunningham.

'We'll wait and see if she was working, too. She might have been out. Let's not wake her. We've got his attention. He'll be eager to please.'

'What do you mean?' said Cunningham.

'He's just looked down and saw two younger women wanting to come in and talk to him. Seoras used to do this sometimes. He'd tell me to speak to someone, usually if they were male. Softer touch. He's right, with certain people it works. You get more out of them if you're from a different sex. I'll never say flaunt yourself. Never put yourself out to be different from you are. When you're with another officer, think about who the suspect or person is going to respond to the best. Macleod would usually talk to the older women.'

Cunningham laughed. 'I never really saw him as some sort of sex symbol.'

Hope shivered. 'No! Just don't!'

The door opened and from the dark interior of the pub, a man emerged in jeans and a T-shirt. He was of a generation above Hope and he smiled broadly despite his unkempt hair. He really had just got up.

'Come in, officers. Do you want a drink?'

'Not at this time in the morning,' said Hope. 'We're on duty, anyway. We just need to ask you some questions.'

'What's going on?' he asked. 'I could smell something in the air when I opened that window. A burning.'

Of course, you could, thought Hope. She hadn't. She'd been out and about for a while and her nose had adjusted to the coarse burnt fragrance on the breeze. The disturbing and pungent flavour was in the surrounding area, the wind having carried it. The fires had been extensive after all, even if they had been in different barns.

'We've got a missing person,' said Hope. 'A Roy Tilbury.'

'Roy? Roy was in here last night.'

'So, we believe. His parents said so. What do you know about Roy?'

'Roy's a regular down here.'

'Is that so?' said Cunningham. 'Mr?'

'Williams. Kevin Williams.'

'How long have you been the owner of the pub?' asked Hope.

'Ten years now. He's one of those egg people. They come down here and have annual meetings and things. They hire

31

the little room up above. I'm not sure what they do. It all seems quite social, in some ways, but recently we've had a bit of bother in the pub with them.'

'Really? Was Roy part of that?'

'Well, yes. With Roy, but the younger generation, mainly. The meetings are usually Donald Tilbury, his missus, and some of the other ones, the Daniels, the Brodies, the older set. You can see that they're not happy with each other, but they wouldn't openly fight how this lot does.'

'So, there's been like punch-ups and stuff?' asked Cunningham.

'No, I'd never let it get to that point. I'm a landlord, not daft. They spend a lot of money in here throughout the year. Keeps me going. As long as they do that, I'm happy enough to cut off any shenanigans at the cusp before it gets too heated.'

'What are they getting heated about?' asked Cunningham.

'I don't really know. It's egg business. They don't seem happy with each other. It's the younger ones mainly, as I said. The Daniels, the Brodies, and the Tilburys—they're the primary cause of it. But then they've had some problems, haven't they? The odd break-in, people harassing chickens. The old guy, Donald Tilbury, was in one day, and he was telling me about it. He put in one of those electronic systems for his hens at night so nobody could access. Now, the thing was that they never used to have that. They would have locked the hens in, yes, but nothing so sophisticated. He told me it was health and safety, but I doubt it. You had to be able to get out as well though, that was key. The hen barns are quite something, apparently.'

'They drink a lot?' asked Hope.

'Real end-of-the-day thing. When it goes dark, the hens will all be inside, anyway. That's the thing, especially in the winter.

32

That's when the farmers get a lot more time off. Then they'll come down. What else is there to do, I guess? Maybe your accounts or whatever. A lot of the work takes place in the summer. Renovations, changes, whatever they're doing. In winter, you're stuck. They come down here.'

'You said Roy Tilbury was here last night?'

'Yes.'

'Was he with anyone in particular?' asked Susan.

The man paused for a moment. Susan looked at him with his short black hair. He had some physical strength in his arms but also had a thinness to him. His nose protruded. In truth, he wasn't particularly attractive, but he was being congenial in answering the questions.

'He was down with that egg crowd, the damnable egg crowd. They were over in that corner. See over there?'

He pointed to a place beside the fire, a fire that was no longer lit.

'They like that. You get the heat from the fire, especially in the winter. There's several of them. Some are quite young, in their teens, up to older people like Roy and some others. You rarely get the older generation, though. Donald Tilbury and that lot. When they do, they maybe come in and have a meal. They'll sit together rather quietly, but also respectfully. The younger generation put the booze down them.'

'What are the rows about?' said Hope. 'You've said they row a lot, but I'm not getting any specifics.'

'I keep telling you. It's the egg business, as far as I can make out. Look, I'm not one to sit and listen to what they're going on about. I get involved when the voices get raised. I'm a landlord to other customers. You don't do this job for long before you can see when things are happening. When they do, they get told to shut it or they're out.'

'Have you ever had to throw them out?' asked Hope.

'Not physically. I've told them to get out and they've gone. But they've had some blazing rows. You wouldn't think the young girls could go at somebody like that either.'

'What about the older ones? You said they come in and they're very peaceful. Have they ever had rows here too?'

'Once or twice. They're the sort of people that when it gets to that stage, they would take it outside. They apologise. Not as a group. Individually afterwards. Different generation. To them, it's not acceptable. Obviously, whatever's bugging them, it's important enough that they still do it.'

'When did Roy Tilbury leave last night?'

'Just before ten. In fact, I think they were all away by ten. Wasn't a late night last night, but then again, it was a weeknight. Got to work tomorrow. There was a bit of drinking going on. I didn't think it was overly feisty last night. No, but they were all out here. Tell you something, though. They're not behind the door looking around the crowd.'

'What do you mean?' asked Susan.

'Don't take this the wrong way, but some of those guys, they're middle aged. None of them have got women. Some of the girls when they come in, well—' The man looked over at Hope. 'I mean nothing by this, but I opened up that window this morning, and you're standing there, Inspector, and your colleague with you. It's very pleasant to look at you. Now, the younger girls come into that group, and again, they're very pleasant to look at. Some of those older guys there, they're not looking at them with, well, "that's a nice-looking woman idea." They're looking with a lot more intent.'

'Intent?' said Cunningham, almost laughing. 'You're saying

they're actually going to make a move?'

'No, no,' said the man. 'I don't know of anything untoward. But they are looking with intent.'

Ten minutes later, Hope and Cunningham had raised his wife, asking her if she knew anything, but she had little more to offer than what her husband had said. Once outside, Cunningham stopped Hope by the car.

'Looking with intent.'

'He was being very polite. They were having a good gawk. They were thinking about what they could do with them, maybe even imagining where their life would go with a younger woman. Makes me wonder.'

'Wonder what?' asked Cunningham.

'Just what the egg business is,' said Hope. They got back into the car. 'I think it's time to call a conference,' said Hope. 'We're going to need to work out a plan of attack. Seems like there are quite a few people to talk to.'

Chapter 05

I t was the back end of the morning by the time Hope had got her conference together. She told Susan to pull together all the details about the Tilburys', Brodies', and Daniels's farms and of their families. Ross was making his way back from the Tilbury Farm and Macleod was coming off the back of a meeting with Clarissa. Prior to them all arriving, the door of Hope's office was knocked and then opened before she could say anything. A man in a rather dishevelled suit, with a tie that hung low from his neck, stood looking at her.

'Detective Inspector McGrath?' asked the man. Hope nodded, and he moseyed his way over.

'Macleod sent me, or rather he called me in. I'm Detective Constable Warren Perry.'

'Did he get you up early?' asked Hope.

'No,' said the man.

Hope cast her eye over his clothing. He looked ragged. His trousers, unlike Ross's, were not creased correctly. They had possibly been worn for a while. A packet of cigarettes was clearly evident within one of the pockets, and even if there hadn't been, Hope could smell the smoke off him from a mile away.

Hope stood up and put her hand out. 'Welcome,' she said. He reached over, shaking her hand, and looking her up and down.

'Never worked for a woman of your age before,' he said. He continued to shake her hand as he continued his survey.

'Over there, in the outer office, that's DS Alan Ross, likes to be called Ross. You know where Seoras is upstairs, and then we've got Susan Cunningham, another DC, just over there at the desk.'

The man turned round and watched as Susan was leaning over. She had her elbows on the table, her backside staring back at the pair of them. Hope saw that Perry was taking a longer look than was strictly necessary.

'Great,' he said. 'Apparently, you used to have Urquhart here.'

'You know Clarissa?'

'Worked with her a while back—not on the murder team, obviously. Seen her on a few cases. Not much to look at, but she knows how to handle herself.'

'Well, I know how to handle myself as well,' said Hope. 'Go through and get yourself a coffee. Ross will show you the desk where you're going to sit. I'm going to do a briefing soon, so you'll be back in here. Macleod will be down as well. You'll come on board, but I don't know how long it's for. At least to the end of this case, anyway. I'll find out for you what's happening.'

'Good, I'm sure it's going to be great working with you.'

As Perry turned away, Hope thought he was deeply insincere. Either that, or he was saying it tongue-in-cheek, commenting more on how she looked.

His comment about Clarissa was unfair. She's an older woman, but she looks well. She dresses up smart. Yes, she was brutal in her

37

approach to people at times.

Hope didn't have time to think any more about it. DC Perry was going to be working with them, so she would have to see how he got on. She went to the door of her office, which had now been closed by Perry, opened it, and called over Susan.

'You nearly ready?'

'I think I've got a good idea,' she said.

'Call them in then, see where Seoras is.'

As if his name was trolled to attract his attention, Macleod walked in through the office door. 'Get me out of the way of that woman,' he said. 'Do you know much about art from the eighteenth century?'

'No,' said Hope.

'I think I got told it all in the last hour and a half. Still not interested in it.' He walked through into her office and sat down at the little round table, then turned back. 'Sorry, am I okay to sit? Are you ready to go?'

Hope laughed. 'Yes, we're ready. I've also got DC Perry here.'

'Trust me, he's good,' said Macleod. 'You might struggle with him, but he's good.'

'Why would I struggle with him?'

'Well,' said Macleod. 'You and Susan, you may, and anyone quiet.' Perry had walked into the office.

'Morning, Detective Chief Inspector?' said Perry to Macleod.

'Morning, Warren. It's Seoras these days.'

'Of course it is, sir. Morning, Seoras.'

Perry sat down at the far end of the table, and Susan came in to sit beside him. When Ross was through, Hope closed the door.

'We won't have Jona joining us. She's still busy up at the farm.

This case could grow arms and legs and certainly, there's many people we are going to have to get round to talk to. There seems to be possible friction amongst the egg community, but I'm not sure how much. I've asked Susan to hunt out who's who, give us an idea of who we're going to interview. Susan.'

Cunningham stood up and plugged a cable into her laptop, so that a picture came up on the screen behind her.

'Egg production around the Inverness area is dominated by three families,' she said. 'We've got the Tilburys, we've got the Brodies, and we've got the Daniels. All very different, and they've got families ranging from the young to the old. All these people would be down in the Drowsy Duck from time to time, though mainly the young people.

'We'll start with the Tilburys. We believe Roy Tilbury may have been in one of the barns and may be our victim. There are two parents living there, Donald and Esme, and they have their son, Roy, who we believe may be deceased, and Jenna. Donald was the owner of the farm for a long time, in fact, still is, but Roy was due to take it over. Donald is heading into his sixties. Esme is up in that range as well. Roy is in his late thirties—been told it's thirty-eight. But they have a daughter, Jenna, who's nineteen.

'I got most of this information from the landlord of the Drowsy Duck. Apparently, Jenna and the younger ones are frequently there, but Roy is also. Roy and Jenna are brother and sister, but quite an age gap. Roy would be taking over the business. Jenna, from what I understand from the landlord, wouldn't be heavily involved. She quite likes her makeup, but really, I need a better picture.

'The Brodies own a large egg farm as well, but the man who started it all off has died and we have widow Lorraine.

She's sixty. She's got a daughter, Peppa, who's approaching forty. Peppa has two daughters, Sarah, twenty-two and Fern, who's sixteen. It's a farm run entirely by women at the helm. Lorraine's known as quite a shrewd customer and a tough one. According to the landlord, Sarah and Fern are extremely good looking.'

'Wow, this is looking up,' said Perry suddenly. Hope and Cunningham stared at him, as did Ross.

'Probably not the team to be making those sorts of comments on,' said Macleod. 'Different day.'

'All right. Of course, Inspector.'

'How well do you two know each other?' asked Hope.

'Warren and I go back to Glasgow days. Worked closely with me on several cases, didn't you, Warren?'

'Indeed,' said Warren. 'It was an all-male team back then, but that wasn't my choice. I'm always happy to work with women.'

There was something in the comment. Was there a sexual tone in it? Was that the way he meant it? Hope wasn't sure.

'Modern day though, Warren. So, let's watch what we say and we'll get on,' said Macleod.

'Can I get on?' asked Susan.

'Of course,' said Warren.

Hope watched how he stared at Susan Cunningham. Susan had a reputation within the station, one that Hope found to be transforming. Once upon a time, she'd be one of those girls who would be out with everyone. She'd have a different guy almost every night of the week, or certainly every time she was out.

Now, however, although she didn't have a regular boyfriend, she seemed to talk about the same people, less about any sort of sexual conquest. Hope thought that she was insecure, and

40

needed to show off her sexuality to be something. She had moved to be an image that certain people, or at least, certain men, would have had her be. It wasn't healthy and Hope was glad to see the change.

'So, the Brodies, as I said, widow Lorraine, daughter Peppa, and then the two daughters, Sarah and Fern. I've spoken to the landlord, and Sarah and Fern were certainly there last night.

'We also then have the Daniels, owners of one of the large egg farms. It's run by Bernard Daniels, who's a widower, age seventy. He's got a divorced son, Clive, who's forty-three, and he's got two kids there. Alexis, nineteen and Steven, sixteen.

'This group of people, together, have been the driving force of egg production in the area for years, but, according to our landlord, they've been openly rowing. The largest farms are the Tilburys followed by the Brodies, but the Daniels have made great strides. They have changed a lot, invested, and seem to have grown, from what I can gather. That's about as much of a picture as I've got. We don't know what the rowing is about. We don't know the state of each farm, and I so far have got no clue who would want to murder Roy Tilbury, if indeed that's him in there.'

'I think we've got to run with the line of inquiry that it is Roy Tilbury. He's not showing up after coming back from the pub. He should be in his house. His parents do not know why he would do a runner, so therefore, let's assume,' said Hope, 'that it's him in there. We need to find out what's going on between the three farms. We'll start off by going to visit the two we haven't for now. It'll give the Tilburys some time to calm down. I'll take Susan and we'll visit the Daniels. Ross, take Warren with you. Go and see the Brodies.

'The key for the visits at the moment is one: find out where they were last night, right through the night, if possible. Find out who was at the pub, what any rowing was about, or what the rows have been about in the past. Two: see if they've got any financial troubles or worries or how that would affect Roy and get their impression of the Tilburys. Three: we'll also need to talk to Jenna because if Donald was handing the farm over to Roy, it's now going to go to Jenna Tilbury, but we'll do that later. Foremost, let's get out and find out who the rest of the egg production families are.'

'Good,' said Macleod. Hope noticed he continued to sit as everyone stood up. Warren looked over at Ross.

'You and me, boss, then,' he said, 'out to a farm load of women. Brilliant, eh?'

Hope threw a look that said that the comment wasn't a good one, whereas Ross seemed to ignore it. Susan was closing down her laptop and as she'd packed it and went for the door, Hope noticed Perry held the door open for her.

'Thank you. That's very chivalrous,' said Susan in a sarcastic tone.

'Well, we're always meant to look out for the little ladies, aren't we?'

Susan shot him a look and disappeared into the outer office while Ross ushered Perry out of the office, the door swinging shut behind them.

'Hold the door open for the little ladies,' said Hope.

'You'll be all right,' said Macleod. 'You're taller than him. Can hardly call you a little lady, can he?'

'Where did you dig him up from?'

'He's good. Keep your mind open about him.'

'Tell him to keep his eyes off my DC.'

'He's from a different time, really,' said Macleod, 'Back in the day, it was an all-male team down in Glasgow. Warren's struggled to change with the times. He's harmless though. I mean, he's not a—'

'What,' said Hope. 'A perve?'

'He's certainly not that. Give him a bit of space, but obviously, don't take any nonsense. He's on the team for a reason. Trust me.'

'I don't really have much other choice, do I? I can't very well send him packing now and ask you to get me somebody else.'

'Well, if you do, I have got nobody currently available, and it'll be me.'

'In that case, I'll make do,' said Hope.

Macleod stood up and went to go for the door.

'Seoras,' said Hope. 'A word.'

'Oh, what?' asked Macleod.

'Do you ever regret not having kids?'

'That's not my first regret,' he said. The first regret is that my Hope died. I think if she had have lived, we'd have had kids. She would have been good with them. Jane would be good with them too, but Jane's too old.

'You're too old as well,' said Hope. 'You can't blame Jane only.'

'I don't,' said Macleod. 'Of course, I don't,' he laughed. 'Why are you asking?'

'No reason,' she said. 'No reason at all.'

'Oh,' said Macleod. 'I regret it, by the way, even with all that happened, I regret not having kids. I see them now, see the connection. Even Ross with his one. Even if I adopted. Instead, I'm, so Jane says, "married to the job." There's this part of me, a part of me she doesn't get back. I think kids will keep you more grounded in real life. Easier to throw away the job one day. I can't. I think we all make titles for ourselves. Mine was detective. It wasn't anything else. You're a detective, too. Be a mum. Be a lover. Be other things, because one day you're going to need to take this cap off and be happy with that.'

Macleod turned and walked out the door, closing it behind him. Hope stood with her hands in her jeans pocket, watching him go. She'd never realised so, until now, just how much of a regretful figure he was.

Chapter 06

'What do you make of him, then?' asked Cunningham as she drove Hope over to the Daniels farm. It was approximately three miles away from the Tilburys but had a better access road.

'Who?' said Hope absent-mindedly. She'd been thinking about the egg farms, realising their proximity.

'Perry, Warren Perry, our new DC,' said Cunningham. 'He's a bit—'

'Not very PC, you mean?'

'Well, he's not really, is he? Quite the obnoxious sort, in some ways. Slapping Ross on the back while visiting an all-woman farm.'

'I did notice,' said Hope. 'Can't very well just pull him to one side straightaway. I want to see if that's just his way of fitting in, trying to get along with the boys.'

'Well, I will not tell you your business,' said Susan.

'No, you won't,' said Hope. It was a little too sharp. After all, this may have been Susan's way of bringing up something she was struggling with, but Hope didn't need the distraction. What she needed was to get deep into this case and find out what was going on.

'Besides,' Hope said to Susan, 'he comes highly recommended by Macleod. Seoras doesn't give me rubbish. He hasn't so far.' She cast a glance over at Susan, who'd flicked her eyes towards Hope and then back to the road.

'Of course not,' she said.

There was an awkward silence for a moment until Hope's mobile vibrated. She pulled it out and answered a call from Jona, the station's forensic officer.

'Just thought I would update you,' said Jona.

'Go ahead, then,' said Hope.

'It looks like there were proper incendiaries inside the barns. All set on a timer. Couldn't have been that long a timer, though. Somebody could have got a card and gone along the complete series of barns. They wouldn't have had to go very far inside, which is why a lot of the chickens weren't disturbed. We have, however, confirmed it is a body inside. They could have been trying to escape, causing the ruckus that the security guard had heard. It's definitely arson.'

'So, what you're telling me,' said Hope, 'is that our victim possibly struggled while inside that barn, which could have caused the chickens to be in an uproar. Yet we have incendiaries planted all along inside every barn?'

'That's correct,' said Jona.

'Do we know if it's Roy Tilbury yet?'

'Not confirmed. Like I say, I can't tell you if it's murder or if he just simply was inside when they all went off. We'll see what we can do about tracing the incendiaries. One thing to note, though, is that the victim didn't seem to be able to get out. They may have been restrained. We're checking the body. From the movement that we've seen inside, because there have been some marks left within the building, they were struggling.

They were not moving freely.'

'In which case it may be murder,' said Hope.

'Like I say, I don't know. All I can say to you at the moment is it was a deliberate fire. I'll send over further details in my report.'

'Thanks, Jona,' said Hope, closing the call.

'I think I caught the gist of that,' said Cunningham.

'Who wants to burn down chicken houses?'

'I don't know,' said Susan.

The car pulled up in front of a large farmhouse. An older, stocky man stepped out, waving at the car as Hope stepped out of it. He spoke politely but strongly towards her.

'We're not talking to anybody today. There's been a bereavement within the community. I'm not looking to talk to any of the press.'

'I'm not the press,' said Hope, and pulled out her warrant card. 'Detective Inspector Hope McGrath. This is DC Susan Cunningham. I'm here to speak to you about the circumstance you alluded to.'

'Oh, right,' said the man. He was wearing some brown trousers with a large jumper over them, which Hope thought very sensible, considering how cold it felt outside.

'Why don't you come in rather than stand out here? It's not really the weather, is it? I'll get some coffee on.' Hope and Cunningham followed the man through into his kitchen.

'I'm Bernard Daniels, by the way. This is my egg farm. My house. I'm afraid it's a bit of a bachelor's pad. I don't have that many women within the house. Just my Alexis.'

'I believe you live with your son, Clive.'

'Yes. Clive's divorced. My wife unfortunately passed away nearly fifteen years ago. Clive's two children live with us.

47

Young Alexis, she's nineteen, and Stephen, who's sixteen. It's not ideal for Alexis. She could deal with having a woman around the place. Well, you know, don't you? We are very different.'

'If you say so,' said Hope, sitting down.

'Apologies for the place, but like I say, I'm working out of it on my own, really, with my wife gone.'

Hope looked around the kitchen, which seemed immaculate to her. It was modern and certainly put in within the last fifteen years. Bernard Daniels ground up some fresh coffee and put on the filter machine before turning back to Hope and Susan.

'Are you both coffee? I am. I can put tea on if you want.'

'Coffee's fine,' said Hope, and the man turned and took down three identical mugs from a cupboard. 'I take it you've heard,' said Hope, 'about what happened over on the Tilbury farm.'

'Shocking, isn't it? There's been a couple of incidences on different farms. I take it you've heard about them?'

'We're catching up, if you'd like to highlight them for us,' said Hope.

'Well, there was an attack on one of the sheds on my farm not that long ago. There were eggs smashed in another one. I think that was over on Jenkins's farm. It's a much smaller affair. We think it's animal rights people.'

'Do you have much trouble with animal rights, though?' asked Hope. 'I thought everything was free range nowadays.'

'Well, it is, but some of these clowns don't like the fact that all the animals are in together. Too many hens all at once.'

'Thousands of them, isn't it?'

'You'll get round about twenty acres of land and sixteen thousand birds together,' said Bernard. 'I mean, they're laughing at the moment. There was the time when we were all told to keep them in cages, but that was never good. We weren't that way up here. Well, not all of us. Now the hens get to come out when they want and run around, before going back into the barns. Some of them don't, though. This is the thing. It's all about having the free range. Farming's different from just having livestock for yourself,' said Bernard.

'That's the thing. Some of these animal rights people think we should go back to owning our own animals. Have chickens running around cities with your own cow in the back to get you your milk? Absolutely crackers, some of them.'

'Have you had lots of problems with them in the past?'

'It's all pretty recent,' said Bernard. 'We were a lot more backward, I have to say. Before Clive was born, I was making enough money for us, but I didn't really run it as a large commercial farm. Still a bit ramshackle. Clive's modernised a lot of what we do, organised the bank loans, brought things forward into the twentieth century.'

'Twenty-first,' said Susan.

'It is, isn't it? Blimey. That far into it. We're still a family-run farm. It's still us. Me and Clive working together; Alexis and Stephen are doing their bit. I think Stephen's probably more likely to want to be in it one day. Clive will have him doing all the exams, getting the qualifications. You didn't get that in my day. You got on by running the farm.'

Hearing that the filter coffee machine was finished, Bernard Daniels poured a mug of coffee for everyone. He then took a small jug and poured some milk into it. A bowl of sugar was also put on the table.

'Anything else I can get you?' he asked. Hope looked up at him. He was a very convivial man, jolly in some ways. Large

49

jowls and thin black hair that managed to somehow cover that head. When he grinned, she could see one tooth he had was cracked.

'That's grand,' said Hope. 'One reason we're here is we talked to some people down at the Drowsy Duck. Apparently, the egg farmers here use it as their local for some meetings.'

'Yes, we use it for the meetings. That's when us oldies are really there. We're not down that often. The younger generation, my Clive, Roy over at the Tilburys, and Jenna, of course. Bit of an afterthought, Jenna, I think. They go down with Alexis. In fact, do you want to talk to them as well?'

'That would be good,' said Hope.

The man toddled off. Hope could hear him shouting outside for Alexis and Stephen.

'Quite a swish little place. You can really make proper money out of eggs, can't you?' said Cunningham.

'So it would seem,' said Hope. 'And modernised, too.'

Bernard Daniels returned to his coffee before a moment later; a sardonic-looking teenager walked in. She had long, mousy brown hair and heavy eyeshadow on. Behind her was a strapping young man, long-limbed but definitely toned.

'This is Alexis and Stephen. These are police officers.'

'My name's Hope. Hope McGrath, Detective Inspector. This is Detective Constable Susan Cunningham. We're over because there's been an incident on the Tilburys' farm. You may have heard someone's lost their life in a fire. It may have been deliberately started amongst all the chickens.'

'It might ruin that farm,' said Bernard. He got quite sad, his eyes heavy. 'I don't care about things we've said to each other in the past. Donald and Esme are part of us, and they deserve nothing like that. He's a proper farmer, like myself.

Poor animals.'

'There're chickens everywhere,' said Susan.

'Getting back to the Drowsy Duck,' said Hope. 'I was talking to your grandfather about it earlier. Alexis, can you tell me, has there been any trouble recently down there?'

Alexis looked over towards Bernard. He turned to Hope and said, 'I haven't heard of anything particular going on.'

'I asked Alexis,' said Hope, 'if you don't mind.'

'Well, at times.'

'Were you there last night?' asked Susan.

'I was there, but it's not what people think.'

'Well, what is it?' asked Susan.

'It's the Brodie Girls.'

'That's the girls from the farm near here?'

'That's right,' said Bernard. 'The Brodie farm. There's Lorraine, she's a widow. Then she's got Peppa and her two daughters, Sarah and Fern.'

'They don't like men looking at anybody else,' said Alexis. 'That's the problem. They kick off about it, try to flaunt themselves more.'

'What about you, Stephen?' asked Hope.

'I don't go to the pub unless I go with Dad or Grandpa.' The young man looked quiet and sullen, too, as he sat down on a chair in the kitchen.

'He's still only sixteen,' said Bernard. 'Not allowed in the pub without someone.'

'Do you two know anything about animal rights activists? People around here having a go?' asked Susan.

'It's a problem for everybody across the industry, isn't it?' said Stephen bluntly. There was almost no form of expression in the statement. 'Even at school, they're all like that. Glad I'm out of it now.'

'They don't treat people right there, do they? Farming is different. It's one thing talking about animal rights, but you've got to have good animal husbandry. You don't just give the animal everything it wants. You've got to look after it correctly. They talk a lot of—well, nonsense,' said Bernard, stopping short of using an impolite word in front of the women.

The front door opened. Hope turned to see a man in his mid-forties stride into the kitchen.

'Hello. You didn't tell me you were bringing women in, Dad.'

Bernard laughed. 'As if. This is Detective Inspector Hope McGrath and Detective Constable . . .'

'Susan Cunningham,' said Susan.

'Delighted,' said Clive, shaking hands.

'We were just asking your children about some rows that were going on down the Drowsy Duck. We've been hearing from some people down there that things have got heated recently.'

'The trouble is,' said Clive, 'and I don't like to speak ill of fellow egg farmers, but they're getting jealous. We've done really well. Business is booming; things are picking up. We haven't always been the big farm. We haven't always been the place that's been on top. Others have been there for a long time, and they don't like it. They don't like what I'm doing. Things have to modernise.'

'That's just something that people struggle with, Clive. We don't need to think ill of them for that. We just have to give them space.'

'If you give them space, Dad, well, then, you go backwards too. We've got to keep going.'

'How well do you know Roy Tilbury?' asked Hope.

'Grown up with Roy around, really.'

'Did he go down to the pub with you?'

'Not with me,' said Clive. 'Seen him in there. He's one of the ones who can be jealous at times.'

'Did you two hear this jealousy?' asked Hope, turning to the younger people.

'He was jealous, all right,' said Alexis. She was staring at her father as she said it. Hope flicked her eyes over towards Susan, who gave a nod back.

'We hear that Roy Tilbury left about ten o'clock,' said Susan.

'That's correct. We all sort of wound it up. We don't stay too late. In this industry you've got to get up in the morning,' said Clive. 'So, we're all out of there, including the Brodies. But Roy was the first one to make a move.'

'Do you have any idea where he would go if he didn't go home?' asked Hope.

'Why are you asking?'

'The thing is, Clive,' said Hope, 'he didn't make it home, or at least if he did, he's not there anymore. He's missing.'

'Do you think it's him in the barns? Do you think it's him that's been . . .'

'I'm unable to confirm that at this time,' said Hope. 'But we know he's missing.'

'Dear God,' said Bernard. 'Donald and Esme, those poor people.'

'Well, I haven't seen him,' said Clive. 'But he's not one to go running off. This is where we're from. It's where we live. Maybe try to look for him closer to home.'

When they left the building, Hope wasn't too sure what had been said to her. There was something in the way Alexis had looked at her dad when she made her comment about the pub.

53

As Susan Cunningham put the car into reverse to spin out of the drive, Hope couldn't quite put her finger on what had been said and why it was bugging her. *It'll come*, she thought. *It'll come.*

Chapter 07

Ross drove his car towards the farmhouse of the Brodies, aware of the husky smell of the man beside him. Not that he was matured, but the smell had definitely been there around Perry for a long time. Ross was picking up on cigarette smoke, but he thought it was embedded in the clothes as opposed to something from a fresh cigarette. The man's shirt must have been over a day old. The tie looked like it had never been pushed fully back up to the neck. It was all very unsettling. Ross was always a man who liked to be clean, wanted to present a pristine image, and Perry just looked sloppy.

'She's quite something, isn't she? The detective inspector.'

'Hope's very good. Worked with her for a long time now,' said Ross.

'It's not an unpleasant view first thing in the morning. But she puts on that serious face.'

'She's a very good detective,' said Ross emphatically. 'She wouldn't be where she is if the boss hadn't thought she was more than capable.'

'You've worked with Big Mac for a while too, have you?'

Most people said Macleod's name with a sense of trepidation

or respect. Very few said it in the sloppy way that Perry did.

'You worked with him before?' asked Ross.

'Back in Glasgow. Used to be an all-man team. All the boys. Not up here. Still, I don't blame him. Wanting to get a few women in, especially the ones he's gathered.'

'Hope and Susan are on the team because of their abilities. Same as Jona, our forensic officer.'

'He's got Urquhart working up here too,' said Perry. 'I can see why he's moved her across. Not quite the same calibre.'

Ross said nothing, ignoring the man as they pulled up towards the Brodies' farmhouse. As they stepped out of the car, a middle-aged woman approached from the house. She wore a pair of dungarees, but they didn't sit sloppily around her. Rather; they were neatly cut.

'Who might you be?'

'I'm Detective Sergeant Ross. This is Detective Constable Perry. We've come to ask you a few questions. You've probably heard about the rather disconcerting incident at Tilbury Farm.'

'Talk of the place, isn't it? Everyone knows about it.'

'Do you mind if we come inside and ask a few questions?'

'Of course,' she said. 'Follow me. I'm Peppa, by the way.'

As she turned round and walked towards the house, Perry reached over to Ross as they followed, tapping him on the shoulder. He leaned in and whispered, 'Tidy enough.' Ross ignored the man.

As they walked into the house, it appeared quaint. *Homely looking, even*, Ross thought. There were a few handmade tapestries on the wall. Here and there, little knickknacks. When they were taken through into a sitting room, it was adorned with photographs. All, strangely enough, comprising mainly women.

'Are you wanting to speak to us all?' asked Peppa. 'Mum's in somewhere. I've got two daughters as well.'

'Absolutely,' said Perry, cutting across Ross. Perry was right. Ross did want to speak to everyone. He wouldn't have said it in quite the same way.

Peppa disappeared out of the room for a moment. Before she returned, two teenagers entered. An older blonde girl, and a smaller, younger, black-haired girl. Ross felt an elbow from Perry. He muttered something about the apple not falling too far from the tree. A bit like their mother.

Ross could appreciate that there was a certain attractiveness about the women, although clearly, they weren't his cup of tea. He was getting annoyed with Perry now. Maybe it was just the way the older men got together, and tried to endear themselves to each other, but frankly, Ross wasn't enjoying it.

Peppa walked back in, announcing that Granny Lorraine would be in shortly. She asked if the men wanted a drink. Ross said no, but Perry said absolutely. Ross then agreed to a cup of coffee as well. It was a little while as they waited for the grandmother to arrive. Peppa was busy with the kettle. She spun round, stared at Perry, and then towards Ross.

'Your man's got roving eyes. Good taste, but roving eyes.'

An older woman with white hair walked in. She had jeans on and a jumper. Rather than go over for a cup of coffee, she approached the detectives directly, looking at Ross.

'We're extremely busy. It's a farm. Whatever it is you've got to say, say it quickly. We're not here for a social chat. You,' she said, looking towards Perry. 'Let's keep focused.'

Ross noted he should talk to Perry later. It wasn't good for him, and if anything, it was an abusive trait. The other women, especially the younger girls, who were excited at

Perry watching them, suddenly became much more attentive to Lorraine.

'I said to your daughter that we were here because of what had happened up at the Tilburys. Roy Tilbury's missing and there was a serious attack on their farm.'

'There've been attacks everywhere,' said Lorraine. 'Not unusual. Animal rights. We talked about it at the last meeting of all the egg producers. They've been ignorant as ever. Some people just don't understand the way farms are managed—why we do things and how we do things. We care about our animals. Don't worry about that. That's one thing that's definitely true.'

'I'm not suggesting in any way you're not,' said Ross. 'Outside of the animal protesters, though, would you say anyone would have a reason to do such a thing to the Tilburys?'

'Everybody got on well with the Tilburys. A lot of the egg families around here grew up with each other. The kids know each other. But I have to say that Esme and Donald got jealous. Especially at the success of the Daniels's farm. They're doing really well over there. Clive gave the old man a good kick. They've come up from not having a lot to being one of the biggest farms around here. That's where a lot of the rowing comes from.'

'Rowing?' said Ross.

'You don't fool me, Sergeant,' said Lorraine. 'You're here because somebody would have told you about how things kick off down at the Duck. Yes, they do. It comes from the Tilburys being bitter at the success of the Daniels.'

'Are you bitter at their success?' asked Perry.

'No, we're fine. We have enough. We're doing okay. I think you need to be looking at animal rights people. Too many chickens harmed with their incendiaries. The animal rights people are daft. They wouldn't just open the doors because they'd get in their heads that we would just put the chickens back in. Instead, they burnt the place down. They actually burnt chickens in the process. You got to look after your animals better than that. That's why you want farmers in charge.'

'So, the rowing down at the Duck doesn't involve you?'

'Sometimes,' said Peppa.

'Sometimes,' said Lorraine, coming across from the door towards Peppa, 'we're getting caught in the crossfire. You can't stand and just have a drink, can you? All our kids grew up in each other's company. We know each other as well, but days have changed and the Tilburys are on their way down. It brings resentment, and that brings jealousy. Look at us. I'm widowed. Peppa's on her own with two daughters here. It's a farm full of women. Even in farming communities, that's not normal. Women on their own, managing, coping, surviving. Most of the others have attitudes like him over there,' she said, pointing at Perry.

Ross noticed Perry stared again at the younger women, but he also noticed that they didn't back away. They weren't horrified. Rather, they were enjoying the attention.

'Your daughters go down to the Drowsy Duck then on their own?' asked Ross.

'There's like three sets amongst the egg farmers,' said Peppa, suddenly. 'There's my age group, around their forties. They are there often. The older set, like mum here, don't go down that often, but they'll be down for the meetings. The younger ones, well, they like to come together and congregate.'

'Is that where things kick off?' asked Perry.

'Are you on about the rowing again?' said Lorraine sharply.

'No, I meant you work hard on the farm,' said Perry. 'At some point, everybody comes together. I'm sure there're relationships built. Must be good to grow up with farming families beside each other, mixing, getting together, forming new families. Farming is a different way of life, isn't it? Good if you're marrying someone who understands and knows what it's like.'

'If you say so,' said Lorraine. 'As you can see, we haven't married. We're all women here and we can cope.'

Perry gave a nod. Ross watched him thoughtfully before broaching another question.

'Roy Tilbury was at the Drowsy Duck last night. What time did you leave?'

'Round about ten o'clock,' said Peppa. 'We all did, really. Roy was first. You don't stay late—got to get up in the morning. When it goes dark, you head down, you have your couple of hours, a bit of chinwag and stuff, and then we all head home.'

'Had supper on for them coming in,' said Lorraine. 'They're up early. We all are up before it's even got daylight. I'm sure you know nothing about that.'

Ross felt a real hostility from Lorraine Brodie, and he was wondering where it was coming from. But he didn't push it. Instead, his interest was drawn to how silent the young women were.

'What about you, Fern?' said Ross. 'I take it, it is Fern. You are the younger one.'

The black-haired girl looked up at him sheepishly. 'I was there, and that's what happened.'

'Who were you talking to last night?' asked Ross.

'Is that really relevant?' said Lorraine.

'It's very relevant,' said Ross. 'I've got Roy Tilbury missing and your granddaughters and daughter were amongst some of the last people we know to have seen him. I haven't asked it for no reason.'

'We were all in a large group last night. The middle-aged ones with the young ones. None of the oldies were down except for Mum,' said Fern. Ross noticed Lorraine turned and gave her a smile about that.

'Like I said, we're very busy,' said Lorraine. 'I'm sorry for the tragedy up there. Roy's a decent guy, but you're barking up the wrong tree here. It will be these animal rights people. It's always animal rights people. Attacking farmers everywhere, thinking they know what they're doing. Girls, get yourselves back out there. Check out numbers three and four barns. Might need cleaning out. See how those layabouts we call workers are actually getting on with things. Peppa, you can see these men out. If you'll excuse me,' Lorraine said to Ross, 'I need to be getting back to running a farm.'

Ross let the woman walk across the room, got past his shoulder until he stopped her. 'Just one more thing,' said Ross. How much do you know about the operations up on the Tilbury farm?'

'In what way?' asked Lorraine.

'The barns—they have a keycard to get in.'

'Most of us put that in because of the animal rights protestors. They're not there to prevent the likes of us. If you know what you're doing, it's very easy to operate.'

'You understand the systems and how they work?'

'Everyone does. It's not complicated, is it? Now, excuse me, Sergeant.'

Lorraine marched out of the room. Ross turned back towards Peppa. She seemed to have an almost regretful smile on her face.

'You'll have to forgive my mother. She's very protective of the family, very protective of me and the girls. She isn't wrong, though. There's a lot of bitterness about the success of the Daniels. They've done well and come from nowhere. Tilburys were on top of the tree for a long time. I'll see you out, though. Otherwise, my mother will get annoyed.'

Peppa walked past Ross, who turned to talk to Perry, but he saw that the man's eyes were once again on the woman.

'Give it a break,' said Ross in a whisper. 'These are suspects, not the candy on a TV movie.'

'Observation is one of the key skills,' said Perry, suddenly to Ross. 'Well, tell me your eyes aren't observing as well.'

Ross shook his head and turned to follow Perry. He was very close behind Peppa.

'Be seeing you again. Thank you for the coffee,' said Perry. Peppa smiled back at him, but then stood at the doorway until Ross had turned the car around and was driving away.

'Fine collection of women, strong one at the top,' said Perry.

'Is that the reason you're still a constable? You can't learn to behave? Follow the codes of the day,' said Ross. 'Clarissa had trouble changing, although she didn't have your eyes.'

'Eyes are made for observing. I'm simply observing. Not my fault if there's something worth observing.' He gave Ross a smile, turned, and pressed a button for the automatic window to roll down. He reached inside his pocket, took out a cigarette, and went to light it up.

'No,' said Ross. 'We don't do that in the car. It's my car. I'm not having it stunk out with smoke.'

The cigarette was returned to the inside pocket, and Perry turned to Ross.

'Well, you're the sergeant here and I guess it is your car, so fair enough. I'll need to pop outside, though, when we get back to the station. Busting for a fag.'

Ross couldn't help but notice the cigarette smell that emanated from the man, that deep nicotine smell. *How did smokers never realise how much they stunk?* Ross moved his window down slightly and then continued quickly back to the station.

Chapter 08

Ross shut the car door and stood in the station car park waiting for Perry to exit the vehicle. The man clambered out, spat on the ground, picked out a cigarette, and lit up.

'I'll be inside,' said Ross. 'Whenever you're ready.'

'Just need a fag,' said Perry. He coughed up some expectorate and continued to stand beside Ross's car, much to the owner's annoyance. It was bad enough having him in the car as he was stinking it out. True, he wasn't smoking in it, but that didn't stop the smell seeping from his clothes into the car's fabric.

Ross marched over to the station door but stopped as he was about to enter. Turning back, he saw Perry standing, watching a couple of female officers get into their vehicle. Ross wasn't happy. The man was like a dinosaur, yet he was twenty years younger than Macleod. Ross knew the boss had his own issues in the past, but these days, he treated everyone with the same respect as everyone else did.

Ross entered the building, continued up the stairs, entering the team's office at his usual crisp pace. He saw Hope was in her office and she glanced up at him as he came in. Susan Cunningham was behind her computer, tapping away as Ross made his way over to the coffee station. He grabbed his mug, went to tip some coffee in and realised that the thermal jug was empty. Without complaint, he quickly ground some fresh coffee, put it into the filter machine, and started it. As he waited for his coffee to be made, he wandered over towards Cunningham.

'How did it go?' she asked. 'How's the new boy?'

Ross thought that was a bit of a strange comment, considering he was older than Cunningham by a significant degree. They were used to having older people within the team. Clarissa was older than everyone except Macleod, but she was young and vibrant in a lot of ways. One of the most dynamic people on the team, if in a rather rough fashion.

'Smoke's all over the car,' said Ross suddenly.

'Well, tell him not to smoke in it. It's your car after all,' said Susan. 'I wouldn't see Hope letting me smoke if I did.'

'He's not smoking in the car; it's just the clothes smell of it—everything smells of it. You come back, want to come up here and get on with things, and he's down having a cigarette outside.'

'I can see why that would bother you, but you're a bit over the top for a first day. The man's only just arrived. Got to cut him a bit of slack, Ross.'

'I'm surprised you're not bothered by him.'

'In what way?' asked Susan. 'We sat in one meeting.'

'He watches women a lot.'

Cunningham almost burst out laughing. 'There's a few of them about,' she said. 'We used to get it down around the lockers. We look at each other, you know.'

'Not like him. He watches. It's creepy in some ways.'

'You find it creepy, but he will not be looking at you.'

65

'It's not the standards we should have,' stated Ross.

'He was a bit off in the meeting. That's just what he's been brought up with. I don't think he realises you're not of that persuasion either.'

'Clearly not.'

'You haven't informed him?'

'No,' said Ross. 'I'm just me. He can take me or leave me as I am.'

'I guess he knows you've got a kid, maybe. Put two and two together and got seven.' Cunningham laughed again.

'You seem too chilled about this. This sort of thing needs nipped in the bud.'

'I've got to work with him. I could be sent out with him. If he says something to me I don't like, I'll nip that in the bud. In the meantime, you're his sergeant. That's the inspector in there, in the office. That's up to you two. When he does something I really don't like, I'll tell you, but before that, I'll tell him.'

Ross nodded, took his coffee cup, went to the machine and filled it.

'Do you want one?' he asked.

'Of course,' said Cunningham. 'By the way, how was the all-girl farm, anyway?'

'Strange, very brusque, wanted us to get back out of there quickly, although the younger ones weren't like that. It was the older woman, Lorraine; didn't feel right. What about yourself?'

'Bernard Daniels brought us in for coffee. Very pleasant in a lot of ways. They said there was a lot of jealousy coming from the Tilburys. Also, there'd been several incidences before; talked about animal rights protesters.'

'We got that. We got that strongly,' said Ross. 'Going to check downstairs with uniform to see what was reported in.

Things don't always get fully highlighted.'

'Good idea,' said Cunningham.

'I'm going to go over to the boss first, though.'

'Just one thing,' said Cunningham, 'the younger ones seem to do the rowing, not the older ones. Trouble at the Drowsy Duck doesn't seem to be from those who are actually running the farms, or at least those owning it. It seems to be the younger ones, the would-be owners coming up, especially the much younger ones.'

'Follow me in a minute,' said Ross. 'We'll talk about it with Hope. I just want to see her for a moment.'

Ross took his cup and knocked on the door of Hope's office. There was a polite 'Come in' and he entered to see Hope looking over some reports.

'I'll bring Susan along in a minute. I just want a quick word with you.'

'Something wrong?' asked Hope.

'Yes, there is.'

'There really is, isn't there?' said Hope. Ross looked at her questioningly. 'You haven't even offered me coffee and you've walked in with your own cup. You don't do that,' said Hope. 'You look after the team always and especially the boss.'

'Sorry,' said Ross. He went to turn.

'No, no; if it's that important, I need to know what it is.'

'Perry!' He saw Hope grin. 'He stinks of smoke,' said Ross.

'Yes,' said Hope. 'And?'

'It's going to go all over my car. The smell is going to seep in.'

'Don't let him smoke in the car,' said Hope.

'I don't, but it's from the clothes, it's from everywhere.'

'Take his car, make him drive. I can't stop the man from

smoking. I can stop him smoking indoors. He's not doing it here in the office, but he's entitled to smoke, and you can't say about how a person smells; that's not on.'

'Well, he does.'

'Look, Ross, you're entirely different, the two of you, very different. It's his first day. What's he like when he is out investigating?'

'He asks decent questions. We've only been out at one place. We'll wait and see how he gets on.'

'That's it. Wait and see.'

Ross wanted to turn away, but he wasn't happy.

'That look on your face says you're not happy with what I've just said. What's actually up?' asked Hope.

'Have you seen how he looks at you and how he looks at Cunningham? He looks at other women like that.'

'Yes, he's very forward with his opinions of women. He's very cheeky in some ways,' said Hope.

'You heard his comment before we left? "Two men going off to the all-woman farm."'

'Yes,' said Hope. 'In some ways, it was quite funny. Not what we normally hear in here. But if it had been Clarissa and Susan going off to a male strip joint for interviews, and Clarissa made the comment, you wouldn't have batted an eyelid.'

'Well, no.'

'Well, no. I'm monitoring him,' said Hope. 'He's only just arrived. I want people to be themselves. If that interferes with business or causes other people to be upset, I'll deal with it. At the moment, you're getting upset for me and for Susan. Susan has said nothing to me. I want to see what he is.

'Is he one of those cheeky men making the odd quip? Then fine. If he's an actual guy who perves on women, I'll step on him. But if he just likes the look of me and Susan—just enjoys looking at women without actually being offensive or upsetting them—he's entitled to do that as I am to look at any man.'

'Okay,' said Ross. 'We'll see how we go, but as long as you know I'm not happy.'

'Alan, I think you made that pretty clear. Has he said anything to you about being gay?'

'I don't think he's realised.'

'I didn't think so either,' said Hope, almost laughing. 'He might be in for a bit of a shock when he finds out.'

'Strange that the boss brought him in. I take it was the boss. You were out investigating, so it wasn't you, was it?'

'No, it's not, but just think of the people that Seoras has brought in before. Susan out there. Susan has a reputation in this station. He brought in Clarissa. Now that is a woman with a reputation, not like Susan's, but that's a woman who is now known as his Rottweiler. You've got to give the boss a bit of credit. If he's brought Perry in, he's got him in for a reason. If part of that's to knock him into shape, fine. However, if it's to knock us into shape, well, then you have to accept that too.'

There was a knock at the door and Hope gave a 'Come in'.

'Sarge said he wanted me to come in here after a bit. Are you done?'

Hope nodded, and she saw Perry entering the outer office behind Cunningham. 'Warren, you want to come in, too?'

Perry entered Hope's office. 'Sure, he said.'

Ross went to fake a cough, and Hope shot a dirty look towards him.

'You don't have to call me Warren. Nobody ever did. It's Perry. When we started, it was all second names. Ross here doesn't like a first name, so don't call me that either. And I'll call you Inspector,' said Perry, 'if you don't mind.'

'I don't mind what you call me,' said Hope, 'as long as it's polite. I just thought we'd bring everybody in. Any quick, initial observations? I was speaking to Alexis. That's the daughter of Clive Daniels. She's interesting. She said all the trouble at the Drowsy Duck Pub seemed to come from the younger ones.'

'That's what we heard,' said Perry. 'Those two girls, over on that Brodie farm, they like themselves; they like themselves a lot.'

'What do you mean, Perry?' asked Hope.

'They like a man to look. They like to think that they're the centre of attention.'

Ross was almost looking the other way. 'Do you concur?' asked Hope.

Ross turned back. 'I don't know, but the trouble certainly isn't coming from the top end. It's coming from the younger end.'

'Well, I think we need to dig deeper. They said that there were animal rights involved.'

'I'm getting onto that, Hope,' said Ross. 'I'm going to look at the computer, go downstairs, pull in the reports, see what's been going on around the farms. It's not beyond the realm of possibility, it's animal rights protestors.'

'It's not animal rights,' said Perry. 'There's something else going on here.'

'I'd agree with you,' said Susan. 'The incendiaries were well planned. We've got someone inside. It doesn't look like our victim could get out. I reckon it's made to look like it's the animal rights. Somebody is trying to pull a fast one on us.'

'Possibly, but Ross, follow that line anyway. Susan, I want you to search Roy Tilbury's room. Take a couple of uniforms with you if necessary.'

'What about me?' asked Perry.'

'You're with Ross at the moment. See what he wants you for.'

Perry nodded, but looked somewhat disappointed at Hope. When Perry turned, walked over to the door and realised that Susan was following him, he pulled the door open, letting her go through.

'Thank you,' said Susan. There was a smile on Perry's face, but it soon disappeared once out into the other office. Susan got her jacket and disappeared downstairs while Perry stood waiting for Ross to come over.

'Get yourself sat down beside the computer. I'll draw up a line of attack to go through,' said Ross.

'Bollocks to this,' said Perry. 'I don't do computers. I'm rubbish with them.'

'Well, I do. This is the method we go through.'

'Fine, let me get out and about then. Let me do what I do well. The security guard, we haven't really spoken to him, have we?'

'We saw him that first night. We have some initial interviews with him. It's all in the case files.'

'But we haven't really spoken to him, properly. I'll get myself off to do that, if you don't mind.'

'You say you don't do computers. How bad?' asked Ross.

'Urquhart's probably better than me. She was when I worked with her last time.'

Ross shook his head. He just wanted the guy out of his way. 'Fine, go talk to the security guard.'

'I'll go see Hagberry then,' said Perry. 'I'll be straight back. You want any lunch brought back? There's a good chippy somewhere round here, isn't there?'

Ross waved his hand. He watched Perry leave the room, glanced over to Hope's office, and could see that Hope was watching the man as well.

She'll have to deal with him soon, thought Ross. *He's too much.*

Chapter 09

Perry drove his car out of the car park, noting that the diagnostic symbol was again on the dashboard. He pushed his finger at it several times, but it didn't go away and he made a mental note that at some point he really should get that looked at. He thought possibly the back left tyre was slightly flat, too.

It had been a funny morning, a surprising one in some ways. He was really the runt of the detectives. So much so, he'd been trawling through some rather dull burglaries trying to make a connection towards one particular thief. He'd just about done that when the call had come through from Macleod.

It'd been a while since he'd worked with Macleod. He remembered him down at the Glasgow station, a very different man now to then. A changed man, and Perry thought it was for the better. Did he have a good woman now? Was he just in a happier place? He'd always seemed so morbid before. No, he was still dull, but now, he was a happy man. Perry could see that.

These days, he had been philosophical about all the things that had happened recently. He'd lost his mind, but Perry reckoned in this job if you didn't lose your mind at least once, something was wrong. You weren't normal.

Perry had been thrown into the mix and in with some people he didn't really know. He'd seen them about the station. Cunningham—that was a nice-looking woman. She'd always had a reputation. Station bike, somebody had said. He thought that was unfair. There weren't many women like that. He wasn't sure Cunningham was.

Susan was one of those women who would attract men because she was good-looking and she was young, but he also thought that she didn't know what she wanted. She seemed to pander to other people, their expectations of her. She could do with being stronger.

The inspector was that. Hope McGrath was becoming a tough nut if she'd survived working with Macleod all those years. Perry laughed. He remembered hearing that Macleod had not been happy when she'd suddenly got assigned to him. He'd commented before about her loose behaviour.

Perry chortled to himself. People were always funny, weren't they? Sometimes so up themselves. Ross was a bit of a conundrum, though. He looked so well-dressed, quite sharp. Perry hadn't really known much about him. He'd never spoken to him, but he was always with those women. Perry had assumed he was a lady's man, but a few of the comments hadn't gone down well. He'd have to work him out. It would take time, but Perry always worked everyone out.

Perry wondered what he was going to have for lunch and debated this for several minutes, wondering if the chippy was a really a good idea. He thought about this until he arrived at the house of Joel Hagberry. It was a small semi-detached and looked neat enough, considering Hagberry was a bachelor. At least, he was not a married man or living with anyone.

Hagberry was that age when 'bachelor' was the term. A term that said 'struggled to get a partner'. He was also working the night shift, checking out chicken farms. It can't have been a job that was well sought after.

Parking the car up, Perry wandered down the drive and rapped on the door before seeing there was a doorbell. He pressed it twice, then four times, all in quick succession.

The door opened before him and a man in a black dressing gown looked back at him. 'Yes?'

'I'm Detective Constable Warren Perry. I believe I'm speaking to Joel Hagberry.'

'Yes. Spoke to your guys already when I was up at the farm.'

'Yes, it's just follow-up,' said Perry. 'Do you mind if I come in? I just want to ask you a few questions about people, really.'

'Okay. I spoke to a Cunningham last time,' he said. 'And a Ross.'

'Yes, they send the good-looking ones out to the initial stuff. It's only the long-term hardy folk like myself that get the follow-up.'

Perry gave Joel a grin, and the man seemed to realise it was a joke. Joel led Perry through to a small sitting room and offered him a seat.

'You wouldn't have a coffee, would you?' said Perry. 'I wouldn't mind one. Been out already today over at the Brodies.'

'Sure,' said Hagberry.

'I take it you know them?' asked Perry.

'Know them all,' said Joel, disappearing into the kitchen. 'You have to meet them. Know who's on the grounds in case you're walking around. I can identify all of them.'

'Yes, I was speaking to that Lorraine Brodie. She's a bit of a—'

'Battle-axe,' shouted Hagberry from the kitchen. 'Oh, boy. Is she tough? She grilled me and what I'll be doing? How I'll be walking around? It's a bloody chicken farm.'

'They had all that bother, didn't they?' said Perry. 'Those animal rights people.'

'Animal rights. They're very clever animal rights people,' said Hagberry from the kitchen.

Perry got out of the chair and followed Joel through, his interest piqued. 'What makes you say that?' asked Perry.

'Come on. Seriously? Never seen them. Not sight nor sound of them. Then suddenly, they've got a coordinated attack. They've got incendiaries that all go off together. Talking to some guys in the industry; animal rights people, they don't do that. Ragtag bunch, really. Also, I tell you, they'd be sitting there saying "Yes, it was us" and they certainly wouldn't have done that to those hens. Animal rights people like animals, don't they?'

'It was an accident. Maybe they thought that the hens would have been all right. Maybe—'

'Doesn't seem right to me. It's egg farming. All free range. Loads of other people they could go at. Public isn't going to like that one, are they? We've got animals in obvious distress. I could see that it would be a big showpiece one to do. But this will get people's backs up. It affects the egg supply to the supermarkets. People will get annoyed. And they've just killed a load of chickens. People are going to get annoyed.'

'You ever been a detective?' asked Perry. He gave the man a grin. 'You could be right.'

I think he's completely right, Perry thought to himself. *I don't know why we're even looking at the line of attack.*

'You were saying about Lorraine Brodie, though.'

'Oh, my goodness. What a battle-axe,' said Joel. 'Always on top of me if I'm doing my rounds. If she's up at all, she's there. Several nights ago, she was out in the dark. The light came on as I moved and suddenly, she was standing there beside one of the chicken barns. "Just making sure I'm getting my money's worth," she said to me. Unbelievable. See, the other owners aren't so bad. They'll see you occasionally, make sure you're there. As long as you're doing your stuff, they don't seem to care. She watches everything.'

'What about the younger members? What about the children? Most of them are teens, aren't they?'

'Yes, they say little to me. Not around the farm and that.'

'What about the Brodie girls? Bet you noticed them.'

'Of course, I did. They're—how would you put it?'

'Wee tarts?' said Perry.

'Yes. In that way that they're looking for you to look at them. I don't mean that every woman is. They are. They distinctly want to be looked at and adored. You can see them looking for your reaction. Sort of women that would photograph themselves and then put it up on their accounts. If people don't click in and say you like them, they get annoyed with themselves.'

'Insecure underneath it,' said Perry.

'Probably alone. I don't get that close. This is a job I'm doing. I'm not that interested in them. I'm not that interested in the people. It's chickens. I don't go inside the barns and get all that chicken shit on my feet. And the smell. Oh, blimey.'

'You work through the night mostly, don't you?'

'I do,' said Joel, pouring the hot water into the instant coffee. 'Milk and sugar?'

'Three sugars, plenty of milk,' said Perry.

'Had to give that up. I was getting too much of it. "Not good," said the doctor.'

'Yes,' said Perry. 'Doctors say that a lot.'

'This job is just how I make my money.'

'What interests do you have?'

Joel took him through to another room, carrying the coffee between them. Opening the door, he clicked on the light switch. Two entire walls had shelves across them, all containing board games.

'Three times a week we meet. If you come through here,' with Joel going to the far end of the room and opening up a small door, 'you'll see the den.'

Perry looked in. There were no computers, but there was a table. You might have thought it was an advanced poker table, except there was a board game sitting out on it. Only not something like Monopoly. This was deeply involved, a massive number of pieces. He thought it resembled some sort of spaceship.

'Mid-game at the moment,' said Joel. 'Had to leave it.'

'How long do these games take?' asked Perry.

'Seven hours into that one.'

Perry nodded. Some people might have thought the guy was sad. Not Perry. He was easy-going. People were entitled to their thing. Live and let live. If he enjoyed it, and others enjoyed it, why not?

'This might seem like a really dumb question,' said Perry, 'but do you get a lot of women playing this stuff?'

Joel laughed. 'I get asked that quite a lot. Mainly by my mum.'

'Worried you will not find someone? I take it you are looking in that direction?'

'Yes,' said Joel. 'Women play this sort of stuff. There's two that come here. There's four of us guys and two in our little group at the moment.'

'Oh, your mum's all right then? I'm not questioning it. I'm quite bad at making social connections, too. Quite happy just sitting on my bum, doing the old gee-gees. Read a lot too. Anyway. Let's get back to talking about chicken shit.'

Joel led him back into the front room where the two sat down in single chairs. The sofa looked untouched, and Perry didn't want to disturb it.

'We were talking about the Brodie girls.'

'Yes,' said Joel. 'As I say, they like you to look at them. I don't bother with them. Fern's going away to boarding school soon. They might have had a bit of trouble with her. They drink down at the Duck. I drink there too, when I drink. I don't go out often. Don't mind the odd little drink. But if you're heading out for a night's rounds and that, they do quite a decent meal.'

'Nobody's accusing you of anything,' said Perry. 'I'm just trying to get a feel for these people.'

'The thing is, all the young ones there, they used to be all over each other. There seems to be more friction. Sarah Brodie is all over the men. She dresses like, well, she dresses like a man would want you to dress if he had you alone. Fern—well, Fern's a better looker. Even though she's only sixteen. She's very, very shy.

'Sarah's problem isn't Fern so much. It's Alexis. The two of them, they're always competing in how they look. They're like these catwalk people. "They don't look at me. Hey, people, look at me!" That's what they're like. Sort of girls that will turn your head to look at them, then when you got to know them, you'd probably turn away just as quick.'

Perry nodded enthusiastically. 'Are the older folks okay with this?'

'No idea. Although Alexis, she always comes in a big coat, takes it off when she arrives. I don't know if she's cold or that, but—'

'Are the girls on their own? Are they teasing the crowd?'

'No, it's not like that. Clive Daniels, Roy Tilbury come down. Stephen, the young lad—he's hanging about, too. They're like a group together. As I said, it used to all be quite quiet, all getting on, but recently there's been a lot of friction. I know the landlord isn't happy. Mentioned it to me a few times. Told me once he'd be happy if we could just boot the lot of them out. They pay for all this stuff, that their folks do, meetings and that. They have a lot of their events in there. The Duck's been the place for years, something like that. Seems to me that things aren't so happy these days.'

'They keep it between themselves? Have you seen anybody from the outside talking to them? Any other influence?'

'I know I only work security,' said Joel. 'And I know I plod around the outside of barns, hoping not to tread in any chicken shit in the middle of the night. But I got into security because I have a bit of an eye for detail.'

Perry smiled. The guy had more of an eye for detail than he probably realised.

'I think the trouble amongst them all is definitely internal. I'm not sure how much is known by the older ones. Alexis in that coat. Clive Daniels and Roy Tilbury are very engaged with the girls. Steven's the one on the edge, which is weird, isn't it? I would have thought Steven would've been the one very engaged.

'Sixteen-year-old lad and them dressed like that. You think he'd be like, "Well, hello there!" Hormones rage at that age. People like ourselves can look at them, know what they were, and turn away because, trust me, they are there for more than just to be looked at. They're dangerous. Very dangerous. The kind of young woman you keep well away from you.'

Perry slurped up his coffee before putting it down. He stood up and Joel got up with him. Perry extended his hand, shaking Joel's, and said, 'Thank you. That's been very enlightening.' He turned to walk away and saw a photograph hanging on the wall beside the door. Joel was there with a young girl with glasses. She was maybe in her mid-twenties.

'Who's that?'

'Emma?' said Joel. 'She's one of the ones who comes to play the games.'

'Lovely. She really is,' said Perry. 'You'll do well there. She looks a lovely girl.'

Joel smiled and led Perry to the door. He heard it close behind him and he walked down to the car. Perry thought back to Ross. He was sitting on his computer, cross-referencing this, doing that. *I think I'm getting the measure of this already, and all I had to do was open my mouth.*

Chapter 10

Perry parked the car up in the station car park, stepped out, and lit up a cigarette. He puffed away, thinking about what he'd just been told. Perry liked to understand people. That's where the magic of the job was. Systems and processes could bring you evidence, but you really got to the heart of the matter by understanding people. That's what Perry believed.

He thought he was beginning to understand the people involved. There were no animal rights involved in this. Something was up. If Roy Tilbury had been murdered, then there'd need to be a reason. The reason might be amongst those young people. That's where he spent some significant time, after all. Still, he would go upstairs and see what Ross had produced. Sometimes the computers came up with something good. Usually not when Perry operated them, though.

Putting out the cigarette, he stomped into the building. Dropping by the canteen before going up the stairs, he munched away on a chocolate bar as he entered the office. Ross looked up from over his desk, but the door to another office opened quicker.

'Perry, have you got a minute?'

'Of course, Inspector. What can I do for you?'

Perry walked over while Hope stood at the door. He entered her office and heard the door close behind him.

'Am I in for a dressing down?' he asked. 'I can think of no other woman I'd rather have do it.'

Hope's face was red as she turned to him. 'That's not appropriate,' she said. 'I've had a complaint about you. You're not fitting in very well and the way you spoke at this morning's meeting.'

'How did I speak at this morning's meeting?' asked Perry suddenly.

'Boys, off to the all-woman farm?'

'What's wrong with that? A joke.'

'Not an appropriate joke. I don't know where you worked before.'

'I worked in Glasgow before I worked up here and I have had nobody complain about my conduct.'

'That's not strictly true, is it?' said Hope. Perry raised his eyes. She had read the reports then.

'It says here that you told one of your senior officers they were a bumbling idiot and if they had any idea what they were doing, they would solve this case in no time.'

'That's correct.'

'They hauled you up for that one. What do you have to say about that?'

'That's true. They hauled me up for it, but what I said was also true. We solved it in no time. Police work's about using your brain, not just following the procedures.'

'Another one says that you thought a lady officer was incompetent.'

'I thought an officer was incompetent, and I told them so.

The fact they were female had nothing to do with it. I've told plenty of male ones they were incompetent, too. This individual decided that rather than accept that they were being incompetent, they would instead take it as, for some reason, I thought females were incompetent. I have thought no females were incompetent because they were female. Trust me, male or female, we can all be as incompetent as each other.'

'I've been told that you've been looking at female members of staff,' said Hope flatly.

'What?' said Perry.

'Looking at female members of staff. Standing in the car park watching as female officers get into cars.'

'And? Have you ever watched a good-looking male officer get into a car? Have you never cast an eye over anyone?'

'It's not the behaviour that we need,' said Hope, her voice becoming sterner.

'You're not into all this PC bollocks, are you?' said Perry suddenly. 'I thought working with Macleod would have you knowing what was what.'

'Just what on earth do you mean by that?' asked Hope.

'People. The way people are, men, women.'

'Like I say, I've had complaints.'

'Well, it's coming from inside this office. It's not you because you're the one addressing me. If it was you, it would be Macleod talking. It's not Cunningham.'

'What makes you say that?'

'Cunningham's used to men looking at her. Cunningham actually feels—not a happiness—a sense of dissatisfaction. She has a rep within this station that's not deserved. If anything, Cunningham's lonely and doesn't know how to form a sensible relationship.'

84

'You've only just met her.'

'And?' said Perry. 'She's not like you. You were like her though, weren't you? Confident now, though.'

'This is not about me. This is about you and your behaviour.'

'Have I misjudged Ross?' asked Perry. 'I was just trying to be funny with him.'

'You may have noticed that Detective Sergeant Ross is not quite like yourself.'

'No, he likes the computers. He's very polite to everyone. Sometimes you've got to get people onside. Sometimes you've got to—'

'He doesn't throw his opinion at everyone all the time, either,' said Hope.

'No, but I thought we were having a discussion. I thought you might want to see my side of it.'

'Ross is also gay,' said Hope.

Perry went silent for a moment, and then laughed. 'No wonder he's uncomfortable.'

Perry grinned back at Hope, which wasn't what she wanted. 'You need to toe the line, though. I don't want to have anything on my watch, you being accused of this, that, or whatever. Keep your eyes on yourself.'

'I observe everything. Observation is the name of the game. Wouldn't you say, Inspector?'

'In that case, tell me what you've observed then. I thought that you and Ross were going to be working on the computers. Ross tells me you disappeared off. Went to speak to our security guard. What did you observe about him?'

'I found out that Joel Hagberry is an excellent judge of character. He's a bit of a gaming geek by the way, but that's good with the crowd we're looking at. He's not swayed by them, calls them for what they are. Sarah Brodie, her sister Fern, Alexis. They're all little tar—'

Perry paused. *Don't say the word tart*, he thought. *She won't like that. That'll be PC nonsense.*

'They're all very hungry for attention, especially from men. And they dress to get it. They're looking for your attention. Dangerous people in that sense.'

'Are you saying that every woman that dresses sexually is out looking for it?'

'No,' said Perry. 'You dress sexually.'

'I've got jeans and a T-shirt on.'

'Boots, leather jacket. You dress to be confident in your body. It's great, but you're not dressing to pull someone in. You're not dressing to grab hold of their attention. These girls are. You've also got people there whose attention can be grabbed. Older men, single.'

'What are you on about?' asked Hope.

'When I worked with Macleod, he said to me, "You have to understand the people first. Get into the characters. See things from their perspective." He's quite brilliant, do you know that? Must be hard stepping into those shoes. Probably doesn't stay out of the way long, does he?'

'Why do you say that?'

'Because it's the game he likes. He thrives being in the chase. DCI at the moment; it's boring up there. How many juicy murders require just him to run the investigation? This one, you're running it. Or did he step away for you? Did he know you needed to step in and take things on?'

'I'm not being discussed here.'

Perry put a hand up. 'Sorry, forgot the PC bollocks. Look, forget the fact that many people don't like me. I say what is

86

and I say it the way I see it. Don't have healthy habits. I smoke, which a lot of you don't like these days. I'll do my best to fit in. You can move me on when you're done, okay? But I'll tell you now, Roy Tilbury's in that barn and it'll be a murder committed by the farmers.'

'About the eggs? About the taking over the farms? Jealousy? What do you think?' asked Hope. 'Ross said there was jealousy.'

'Maybe, but it won't have anything to do with the farms. The farmers and their families, not the businesses. Is that all?'

Hope nodded. 'Make sure you toe the line.'

'Ross is gay,' laughed Perry. 'That's cracking. That is so good. I just thought he had something stuck up his arse, and that's why he didn't laugh. He's actually offended for you. Oh, well, live and learn.'

Perry disappeared out to the office, and Hope returned to her desk. Just as she sat down, there was a knock at the door. She looked up to see Macleod on the other side of it. She waved him in.

'Close the door behind you,' said Hope. 'I need to talk to you.'

'Oh, the case is not going well?'

'The case is fine. Perry! I've got Ross on to me about Perry, complaining. Finding him hard to work with. This is Ross.'

'Yes,' said Macleod. 'I can see how that could happen.'

'What do you mean, "You can see that?" This is Ross, sort-everything-out Ross, getting-everything-done Ross, by the book.'

'Yes. As I said, I can see that.'

'Why did you stick Perry here? Was he seriously the only person you could get?'

Macleod walked over to her desk and started to go round the

side of it, and then asked Hope, 'May I?' Hope nodded and she joined him beside her chair. He was looking out the window.

'The best view in the place, this one. The best view. I look out of my office now and it's rubbish. I look out and I want to be back here. This chair. Do you know that? I'm upstairs now, away from you all. When you come in, people make coffee and it's all very formal. I used to hear Ross making the coffee. Ross would bring me the coffee, well made, just how I liked it, before I had even asked.'

'He didn't bring me coffee today. Came in to complain about Perry and he didn't even bring me coffee. He had one for himself though.'

Macleod chortled. 'Really? Good.'

'What do you mean, good?' asked Hope. 'Perry's a handful. Ross said he was staring at female officers getting into their car.'

'He had an eye for women. Always. Did you know he reads poetry? He can recite poetry back to people. A lot of love poetry as well.'

'What are you on about, Seoras?' asked Hope.

'It's been half a day,' said Macleod, 'and you're complaining about him. You're saying he's this, and he's that.'

'He told me not to go on about all the PC bollocks.'

'Yes. You see; that's why I feel for him.'

'I looked up his record. He called a female officer incompetent.'

'No,' said Macleod, 'he called an officer incompetent. The report highlighted that she felt he'd said this because she was female. He didn't call her incompetent because she was female. He called her incompetent because of the case and the way she handled it. I know this because I dug out everything from the case. I looked at it and yes, indeed, she was incompetent.

'Because I've said it, you are quite happy now that she was incompetent and you're thinking maybe you got that wrong. You'll be thinking about all the other things and justifying why you're right with those. Take time and get to know him. He's brilliant. He's exactly what you need.'

'He's frustrating, he's annoying, winding up Ross as he starts out on being a sergeant.'

'Yes, he is, and the first thing you did was take it off Ross and try to deal with it. Ross was out with him, I take it.'

'I took Cunningham and Ross went with him.'

'Why?' asked Macleod.

'Well, because I work well with Cunningham. Cunningham and I get on well. I'm in the middle of running an investigation. I want to be—'

'What? Comfortable? So, you gave him to Ross instead. Did anybody tell him that Ross was gay?'

'No,' said Hope.

'What did he do when you told him? Because I take it you've informed him of that after Ross complained about what he was doing.'

'He chortled, he laughed, said he couldn't get over it.'

'Look, Perry will learn. You should have dumped him right back on Ross and told Ross to deal with it. He's a sergeant now, and when you're a sergeant like you were, you had to deal with people. You've taken charge of those who are beneath you. Ross is beneath you now. You're an inspector. You're not here to deal with all the problems; you're here to make sure that the case runs smoothly, and it gets solved.

'People need to work with each other. You get your sergeants to make sure the team is functioning on that level. If it comes up to you, that's a big problem because your sergeant isn't handling it. Tell him, "I will not handle your problems. This is a matter of teamwork. You sort the help. Handle Perry. I got you the right person. You make sure he fits in. You make sure he's comfortable and everybody can work together.""

Macleod turned and walked away, back out the door, but stopped.

'You complained about Ross not bringing you coffee. You didn't offer me one. Normally, you would offer one. Don't be knocked off kilter by somebody else coming onto the team. Teams change all the time. It's your team, you make it work. If you haven't got time, get your sergeant to make sure the teamwork's happening. Delegate, Hope, delegate,' said Macleod as he walked out the door.

She stared after him, her cheeks red. Sometimes he could be so frustrating.

Chapter 11

S usan Cunningham stood inside Roy Tilbury's room with her hands on her hips, pondering. She had gloves on, careful not to disturb anything as she made her plan of attack on how to deal with the room.

There was a double bed on one side of it, a working area further in, and then wardrobes and sets of drawers on one side. The decor was simple, manly, she would have said. Nothing fancy, just steady, dark male colours. She certainly wouldn't have had her room like this.

Susan liked a bit more vivaciousness, a bit more style, something with curves. The room was laid out functionally. There was a bed for sleeping in. Across from that, all the clothes were ordered in a wardrobe and in drawers. Then there was a work area with a filing cabinet, printer and a laptop. It was almost like an extended office area. Clearly, he would work elsewhere as well, but this looked personal.

As she searched through, Susan couldn't find anything that said Roy Tilbury did any farm work here. It was a little oasis where he regularly lived his daily life. The laptop she unplugged and bagged it up to take it in for analysis. She then worked her way through the desk that the laptop was sitting on, opening the drawers.

Susan searched through finding various books, some on relationships, some on hunting and animal practice, and other basic novels, sci-fi mainly. She continued to hunt down through the drawers, but was aware somebody was standing in the bedroom's entrance. She turned and saw Esme Tilbury looking at her. The woman's eyes were narrow.

'Can I help you?' asked Susan.

'I just wanted to see you were all right.'

'Okay, well, I'm fine. You can leave me. I'm sure there's plenty to get on with at the moment. I'm just seeing if there's anything to give us a clue where Roy may have gone.'

'Roy's in that barn, isn't he? You haven't said yet. Are you holding that from us?'

'No. If the forensic team comes back to say that Roy is in there, you will know. We will tell you straight away. We don't hold back that from you. At the moment, we have a body and we cannot yet positively identify it. We have Roy's records and the forensic team will look to match up and see if the body is Roy's. I'm sorry for your wait. I'm sure it's horrendous, but they have to do the job right.'

Susan was almost going to finish with, 'There wasn't much of a body left,' but she was more sensitive than that.

'Can I assist you?' asked Esme.

'No, it's fine.'

'I know where most of his stuff is.'

'That's exactly why I don't need you to assist me,' said Susan. 'I need to do this. I need to be looking at things that your eye doesn't look at because you're so used to seeing his stuff. You'll lead me down to the obvious. Sorry, it's why we do it. That's why we do it the way we do it. If you'll return downstairs or go somewhere else, it'll be really appreciated. I'm sorry to chase you, but it is what I have to do.'

Susan turned around, opened another drawer, and looked through the different books that were there. She stopped and turned. Esme was still there.

'I'm sorry, I must insist,' said Susan. She stood up, walked over, not quite brushing Esme out but guiding her into the hallway beyond. Susan shut the door behind her and returned to the drawer she was searching. As she got to the bottom drawers of the many that are beside the desk, she found a loose scrap of paper at the bottom. It was underneath several files shoved well to the back. There was a hospital appointment written on it. It was from a diary page; she was sure of it. Susan turned and found the diary again. The back page was ripped out. Clearly, this wasn't meant to be seen.

As she was placing it inside a bag and dropping it into her pocket, she heard the door opening. She turned to scold Esme, or at least guide her out, but young Jenna was there.

'I'm sorry. I have to ask you to leave. You see, I'm doing a search and I need a bit of quiet.'

'Something was up with Roy,' said Jenna.

'In what way?'

'I don't know, but something was up with him.'

Susan got up off her knees, walked over to the door, and closed it. 'Do you mean he was ill?'

'He wasn't quite himself, but I don't think he was ill because he just seemed a little perturbed. A bit focused in on something.'

'How well did you know your brother? Is this something you would spot normally?'

'Roy's older than me. I didn't really grow up with him in

that sense,' said Jenna, 'but I've been around him long enough to know when he's hiding something, when something's bothering him. Was wondering if you'd found anything that said it. I wondered if he committed suicide or—'

'Why would you say that?'

'Well, he's in that barn, isn't he?'

'We don't know that for certain,' said Susan. 'I was explaining to your mum that until we get definite proof, we can't say anything. Obviously, with the fact he's missing and having found a body, it's not a good situation.'

Jenna's eyes were welling up with tears. 'I asked my mother if something was up with Roy. She said I was imagining things.'

'What sort of person was he?' asked Susan. 'I'm looking at the room. It's definitely a man's room.'

'Roy didn't have a clue when it came to that sort of thing. I went out with him and picked a lot of this. That's why it looks stylish. Yes, manly. Nothing too exciting. Roy wouldn't have that.'

'Was he lonely?' asked Susan.

'Not really,' said Jenna. 'I don't think so. He was always obsessed with the farm. It got more difficult, though. Things seem to be much more heated than they used to be. I blame the supermarkets. They drive at us. Everything nowadays is price down, meaning it's harder to make money.

'It used to be, according to Grandpa, that the egg production was easy. You never made billions, but you made enough to support your family and live. It was wonderful, that local selling. He's long gone, of course, now. I think Dad and Mum find it harder. Money isn't the same. Developments, equipment, machines, everything just seems to have become much more driven. And not driven for animal welfare. I get why a lot of these attacks happen,' said Jenna.

'It's not the same today. What does a chicken really want? They want to be sitting in a small group. There are no cockerels with the hens. Normally, a cockerel has a brood of hens around him. He steadies them and they do things for him. They see all of them being born. They raise their young. Here, it's for production. It's not the same.'

'Are you a secret animal rights activist?' asked Susan.

'I was brought up as a farmer. I have animal welfare in my heart,' said Jenna. 'So did Roy. He was never truly happy with the big barns. When I get to whatever stage in life and maybe get married, I'm going to have hens myself. We'll have cockerels, but we'll do it in small batches.'

'You never fancied running this farm?'

'No,' said Jenna. 'Not for me. In truth, that was okay. I'm an afterthought, maybe even an accident. Not that Mum and Dad ever treated me like that, but Roy's a fair bit older. Mum did well to have me. Some couples would have said no. Would have aborted a child at Mum's age.'

'Is there anyone particularly close to your brother?' asked Susan.

'Do you mean as in a relationship? No. Outside of that, it's probably me. Roy didn't have lots of friends and those he did were like pub friends. People you'd say hello to but not people you'd confide in. He didn't even confide in me that much. Quite an independent man. Not that there's anything wrong with that. It's just I always felt most people didn't really know him. Maybe I didn't either.'

'Did he ever keep any work stuff in here?'

'This was his personal space. If it's in here, it was important to him. The business was important too, but he kept that separate.'

'Thank you,' said Susan. 'I appreciate it, but I really need to get on and search this place and I can't do it with somebody looking over my shoulder.'

Jenna nodded and left the room, leaving Susan on her own. Two minutes later, the door opened, and it was Esme.

'I said before—'

'You let my daughter in here. She was talking.'

'I had a question for her,' said Susan, 'about the room decor. She answered it.'

Esme stared intently at her before Susan gently took her, leading her back out of the room again. The woman was grieving. Of course, she wanted to know. She wanted to find out about everything.

Susan continued with her search but pulled out nothing else unusual. She looked again at the hospital appointment, written on a diary page and placed at the bottom of the desk drawers. *Who was it for? Was he dying? Had it been suicide?* Satisfied she'd searched the room, Susan left it and disappeared downstairs to find Esme in the kitchen. The woman was sitting with a cup of tea and as Susan came over, she looked up intently.

'Did you find anything?'

'I've completed my search,' said Susan. 'Would you have the local practice number for Roy? I take it he went to the doctor locally.'

'We're all on the local doctor's list. Certainly, I'll get you the number. Is there any particular reason?'

'Jenna just said he was under the weather.'

'No, Roy was in good spirits. He hadn't been near the doctor,' said Esme.

'If I could have the number anyway, though. I need to tick

boxes and say I've checked this and I've done whatever. Just the way investigating works.'

'Of course, of course, you can,' said Esme.

She came back two minutes later with a number written on a piece of paper. Cunningham made a note of it. She noticed Jenna was hovering down the hallway, but she couldn't talk to the girl easily now, and anyway, she didn't feel she had that much to say. She'd check up this doctor line, though.

Why would you keep an appointment so secret? If you were a tight family and you were ill, wouldn't you tell them? Why would you go and commit suicide? Who was benefiting from that? Jenna? Jenna didn't want to run the farm apparently. Was there something else that Susan just couldn't see at the moment?

She thanked Esme for her time and said they'd be in touch as soon as they had any news on the forensic side of the investigation. Susan placed a call into Hope, but it was picked up by Perry.

'How's things? Enjoying your first day?' said Susan.

'I'm finding Ross hard to work with. You haven't been here long, have you?'

'No, I work with the boss, mainly. She keeps her eye on me. Must have decided she couldn't handle two of us.'

'What did you need?' asked Perry.

'I'm calling the boss to say I've found a note hidden away by Roy Tilbury. It's got a hospital appointment on it. It's not saying who the appointment's for, no details, but important enough to be hidden away. No time on it either. I need to find out what it's about. Seems strange for it to be hidden away so.'

'I've been out to see our security guard, and he's convinced me that something's happening within the group of farms. He doesn't think there's any animal rights activism going on at all.

Thinks it's all happening somewhere else.'

'Interesting. Jenna, Roy's sister, doesn't want to be on the farm long-term. Just wondering where it's all heading. Anyway, I'll be back soon,' said Cunningham. 'I just need to check out what's happening regarding this appointment. That'll take me to the end of the day. Tell the boss I'll catch up with her tomorrow.'

'Good stuff. Will do. See you later.'

'I'll have to catch you for a drink sometime,' said Susan. 'You look like somebody who knows how to drink.'

'Absolutely,' said Perry. 'I'll be delighted to.'

Susan put the call down and wondered what was going on with Perry's mood. He didn't seem as alive as he did earlier on. Not until he mentioned about going to visit the security guard. She'd have to get to know him better. After all, they were both DCs.

Patterson had moved on. She never really got to understand him. That wasn't surprising, given the trauma he'd gone through. Perry would be different. If they were both going to be the bottom rungs in the team, she better make sure they were strong ones.

Chapter 12

Bernard Daniels woke up in his room, feeling somewhat agitated. Those police officers had come, asking questions about the Tilburys and about the other egg farms. They'd asked them nicely, of course. In truth, they were pleasant on the eye, even for an old man like himself. His now-deceased wife would have told him to get real. It was probably the conceit of every man that they thought themselves attractive to whatever age of a woman.

He laughed at himself in bed, rolled his shoulders, and stretched his back. *What time of the morning is it?* he thought. He looked over at the electric clock, a relic by today's standards. One his wife had bought him, that he wasn't prepared to give up. Half past four. It was still dark outside. The morning hours, a little away yet.

Something was bugging Bernard. He didn't know what. Maybe everybody was a little unnerved, a little off-kilter. Especially with Roy Tilbury missing. That body had been found in the barn on their egg farm. *It's a terrible business,* thought Bernard.

He hadn't seen eye to eye recently with the Tilburys. He wouldn't wish it on anyone. Not your son or your daughter.

You expected it with the older people. You expected to see your parents go before you. Your aunts, your uncles. Never your children. It was hard enough seeing the wife go, albeit that she'd been riddled with cancer for a couple of years. In the end, it was a godsend, taking her away from the daily pain she was feeling. It was hard. Very hard.

As he lay there, Bernard thought he could hear something. Was that squawking? Was he just imagining it? It was funny what things did to you at this time of day. You didn't hear the chickens very often from the farmhouse. This was the early hours of the morning, and it was deadly quiet. His bedroom window was slightly open, too. Just letting in a little draft. Bernard liked it to be cooler in the bedroom. These modern houses kept the heat so well, too well for him. He was always boiled alive under a duvet. He liked the fresh air, and it helped with his breathing.

Was that the chickens again? Something seemed strange. He wondered if Clive could hear it. After all, Clive would be the one to go up and check them.

Bernard threw back the duvet and swung his legs out to one side to stand up on his feet. Standing still for a moment, he waited until he was steady. Then he tottered out into the hallway, blearily looking for his son's room. He had no slippers on but the thick plush carpet meant that he didn't feel any cold as he made it to Clive's door. He gave a quiet tap and opened it.

Clive's bed lay unmade. *That's strange*, thought Bernard. *He was out last night.* Bernard had gone to bed before he came back. There was nothing unusual about that, though.

He padded on into the room, pulling back the covers just to check. No, there was no heat in the bed. Nothing. This

100

bed hadn't been slept in. Then an idea struck Bernard. Maybe Clive was worried about the chickens. Maybe he'd gone out to sit close by, keep an eye in case those animal rights people came.

No point in doing that though, because that's what they paid the security firm for. If there were any animal rights people about, then the security people should take the brunt of it, not Clive.

Bernard turned and wandered back to his bedroom. He thought about going to see Alexis, or maybe even Stephen. They'd be sleeping. You could never wake a teenager in the morning. They were as grumpy as hell. No, he'd get on some boots and have a look. Find out what was what.

Bernard pulled his boiler suit out of his wardrobe, found some pants and socks and slowly dressed himself. Trying to warm up; underneath the suit, he had a large, thick aran jumper on, corduroy trousers. Then he walked in his socks down to the kitchen before putting on his boots.

He stepped outside the back door and the floodlight came on, momentarily blinding him. It occurred to him he should really get a torch for the walk-up. He took his boots back off, made his way into the kitchen before returning, now with a torch in hand. He lit it and walked up towards the first of the barns that housed the hens. It was silent around this one. Exterior lights coming on as he approached.

He walked on past it, round to the next one where he could hear hens. They were quieter, though, not the way it had been when he was lying in bed. Had he been imagining something? Maybe so. But Clive's empty bed bothered him.

Where was he? He could contact him on the phone. Bernard remembered that he'd left his own phone by the bed. He hadn't brought it with him. Even after all these years, modern technology bothered him. It never came as second nature. The teenagers never left their phones anywhere, permanently a part of them. With Bernard, it was a daily case of where is the blessed thing. He wasn't going back now.

He'd walked up to the barns, and he'd keep going. Bernard walked on with the lights illuminating as he walked past each barn. Most of the hens were quiet, except the one barn towards the end. It was sat off to the side.

The barns had been arranged in a neat order, except the land around this one hadn't been right. So, the barn had been pushed back slightly. It was towards the edge of their land. As Bernard approached it, he heard the chickens, while not in distress, were certainly restless. Something was bothering them.

Bernard reached into the back pockets of his boiler suit, finding the keycard. He carried two or three because he was always forgetting them. Always laying them down somewhere. Blessed pain, anyway. Another thing that had been put in because of these so-called animal rights people. Why didn't they get off their own backsides and do some farming? Show everybody how to raise animals properly instead of running around and causing chaos.

Farmers looked after their animals. They cared for them. Words like livestock didn't mean that they didn't want the best for them. Chickens here had a good life. They weren't pestered by dogs. Didn't have to keep out of the way of anything. They got their own place. That was quite the change from what it used to be. Scraps chucked out the back.

Everything for them nowadays, from vaccination to food, to the temperature inside the barns. Everything was there. Water too. Took little to satisfy a chicken. The only thing the hens didn't have was a cockerel. Yes, after a year or two, they were gone, their working life done, but that was business though, wasn't it?

He remembered when he was a boy. The hens kept going until they died. Until times were rough enough to need one for the pot. When you grew up on a farm, two things came quickly to you. Pests were pests and needed to be eliminated. You didn't feel for them. Animals also died. Sometimes you could feel for them. Whatever happened, you did it quick, and you made sure they didn't feel any pain. Hens being dispatched once their eggs were no longer laid on a good rate was just part of the business, something to be accepted.

He wasn't living back on a small farm anymore, a couple of dozen eggs taken down to the local shop. His father's farm had not just been eggs, most farmers back then did a range of stuff. These days things became more and more specialised and the Daniel's egg farm was no exception. His father had geese as well. Bernard liked the goose eggs. They were bigger, slightly different flavour, too.

Still, he digressed. Something was going on inside the barn where he could hear the flapping of feathers. This time of night, the lights weren't on; they were in their dark time. Nighttime, not simulated, but given to them. Something was making them restless; something was bothering them. He had to go in and see.

It had been a while since he'd been up here in the middle of the night. Clive always did it. He told him he was an old man and, therefore, as his son, he should do it. As soon as Stephen became of age, he'd send Stephen up.

Bernard got up close to the door, put the smart card in front of it, opening the door, and then took a step back. The lights were on. *Why were the lights on?*

Hundreds of little heads turned towards him. Bernard didn't have the best eyesight, and he tried to keep his eyes down from the blinding light in front of him. He thought there was a blurry image down to the far end of the barn. He reached around the corner, slapped the override on the lights, killing them. *It'll mess up the chicken's routine having the lights on at this time.*

Everything was carefully controlled, the daytime, the number of hours they had on the move. They should be resting now. Carefully, Bernard closed the door behind him and flicked on his torch. There were a few clucks sounding agitated and annoyed as chickens stepped out of his way. He had the beam held down, watching them as he stepped, ignoring the poo on the floor, his big boots slapping their way through it.

With the torch focused down, Bernard watched his feet, for it would be very easy to slip. Slip, bang your leg, crack your head and you're lying here, shouting for someone to come and help, with only chickens coming up close to annoy you.

Slowly he waded his way through a wave of chickens that parted, much slower than Moses got that Red Sea to move. As he came up towards the far end of the barn, his torch caught something on the edge of its light. He thought there were Wellingtons there at first, but no, these were ordinary shoes. Shoes in the air.

Bernard's mind scrambled. Shoes. He recognised the shoes as being a pair very similar to Clive's. Shoes in the air. How can shoes be in the air? He took a step back, looking up, the torch moving its way up: a set of trousers, then a shirt. Then a rope around the neck and a face looking down at him. He recognised it instantly.

Although Clive's eyes were closed, Bernard saw his son hanging, suspended by the neck. Part of him stepped back in horror. Another part, surprisingly to him, wondered how Bernard had been up there. The torch followed the rope, saw it go over a beam and come down to be tied at about chest level over towards the far wall. Bernard's mind snapped back, the torch going up again, and he looked intently into Clive's face.

Bernard stumbled backwards, caught a chicken and ended up landing on his backside. Feathers flew, clucking begun, and Bernard found himself fighting to get past the panicked throng of hens. He lifted himself up off the ground, raced over, and hit Clive with his hands.

'Clive. Clive,' he shouted. He threw his arms around his son's legs, tried to drive him up.

He needed to cut him down. Quickly Bernard looked over at the far wall. That's where it was tied. He ran over, but the thick rope was tied tight. He reached inside his boiler suit, taking out a knife. It wasn't a thick one, but it would do.

He cut hard at the ropes, pushing down with all his might. He watched as it frayed, the first couple of strands, then most of the rest, until he got down to the last few. Bernard pushed hard. The knife slipped through, and there was a loud thud as Clive fell to the floor. The chickens went ballistic again in the dark, but Bernard ignored them, charging in towards his son. He reached down, shaking him.

'Clive! Clive, are you okay? Clive! Talk to me, please talk to me!'

His hands shot up towards Clive's face. Clive was colder than he should have been. There was no movement from his chest. Bernard leaned down, listening to Clive's mouth, but he could hear no sound. There was no breathing. He needed to call for an ambulance.

Damn it, damn it, he thought. *The phone, it's back at the house*. Then something struck him. He patted Clive's pockets and pulled out Clive's phone. He dialled 999 on it, as Clive had told him in any emergency, the phones would go ring 999 with no need for the correct network provider.

'Which service do you require?'

'Police, ambulance. My son's hanged himself.'

The police operator then took Bernard's details, advising they were on their way, and Bernard collapsed down beside his son. He shone the torch on the face of Clive Daniels, his one and only son. His face was motionless, the body limp. Something within Bernard told him to get Clive breathing again. He pushed down on his chest; he blew air into his mouth, but he did not know what he was doing. Bernard had to try. He had to do something.

When the first police officer stepped inside the barn, it was with Stephen behind him. The young man had to get a card, and now that the door was open, he told the police officer where the light switch could be found. The lights went on.

Chickens clucked and cackled, feathers flapping here and there. In the middle of them, sitting on his bottom, his son's head on his lap, being stroked ever so gently, was Bernard Daniels. Someone had killed his son. The man didn't know why.

Chapter 13

Hope lay in bed, John by her side, snoring away. She'd been awake now for maybe half an hour. It wasn't the case that was bothering her. Not Perry either. It wasn't the fact that Macleod had basically told her to deal with things when she'd been looking for help. But he had something he wanted her to deal with, and he was right. She was the DI; it was her team, and she needed to handle it. If that meant in the long run that Perry wasn't there, and she had to find someone else, then that was what it was.

She'd taken the step up and she'd known Seoras for too long now. He wouldn't have brought somebody in deliberately to disrupt the team. Perry was in there for a good reason. One: he could help with the case. Two: he may even help build up the team, though she couldn't see how.

These things weren't on Hope's mind. What was, was the silence of the house. She rolled out of bed in her t-shirt and knickers, one of the various combinations she'd taken to wearing in the last couple of years. John slept in boxer shorts. She remembered that this differed from when they'd started. When they'd started, there wasn't anything under the sheets, no material, just the pair of them. *Maybe that was the start of all relationships*, she thought.

She walked over to the bedroom door, out to the hallway, and down to the kitchen. Ross had told her a week ago about having to get up in the middle of the night to his young son, having to comfort him. Hope thought how wonderful that must have been, to have held someone so small in your arms, to have their total trust and devotion aimed at you.

She looked at the kitchen table. It was wooden, nicely done, but they'd never really seen anyone around it, just John and her. They would sit around one corner of it. Part of her wanted there to be a whole family around it. That was the problem. It was time. She'd decided.

Family. She wanted kids. If she didn't, this police life would take it away from her, surely. 'There was never a good time,' John had said to her. He was right. There wasn't. You just had to make the time. Hope strode out of the kitchen, marched up the hallway, and through the bedroom door, directly to the bed. John was still asleep, but she reached down and kissed him deeply. He almost coughed, waking up, causing her to laugh.

'What's up? What's the matter?'

'Switch the light on,' said Hope. She saw John's hands wander out to the bedside table. He flicked on the light and looked up to see her.

'What?' he said. She reached down, took off her knickers and held them up in front of her, before throwing them to one side.

'This,' she said. She reached down, pulled her top off, and told him to move aside. 'It's time,' she said. John's eyes widened. The adrenaline rushed through Hope. Then the pager for the on-call detective sounded its devilish beeps through the night.

'No!' shouted Hope. 'No! No! No!'

Scene break, scene break, scene break.

Hope's mood was foul as she drove up towards the Daniel's farm, but she knew she needed to calm down. Clive Daniels was dead. The desk sergeant had said he'd been found in his father's arms inside one of the barns. Jona was already on her way up and, as Hope approached, there was the usual cordon and circus of flashing police cars.

As she approached the house, flashing her warrant badge around, despite the fact that everyone knew her, she hoped the team would turn up soon. Walking in through the front door, she took a moment and looked back out into what was now becoming the morning sunrise.

It took away from you, the job. It always grabbed you, grabbed you when you didn't want it to. John had said he'd understood, but he had disappointment in his eyes, almost as much as she had. She'd wanted to say to him, I'll be a couple of hours and then I'll be back. She knew that probably wouldn't be true. Two people were dead now. It could be a couple of days before she got any sort of home time.

Putting on her game face, Hope went further into the Daniels's homestead again, to the kitchen. Bernard was sitting, his arms around Alexis and Stephen. The mood was sombre, and the only sounds were the sniffing of Alexis and Stephen. Bernard's face had the tragedy written all over it, but he didn't weep. Instead, he looked hard at Hope.

'What is this?' he asked. 'Why Clive? Clive did nothing. He just ran an egg farm. Clive was good. These two need him.'

'I'm sorry for your loss,' said Hope. 'I know this doesn't seem

109

like the right time, but I need to ask you some questions. We need to move quick in case there was any foul play at hand.'

'It is foul play,' said Bernard. 'Clive wouldn't leave these two. Not like that. Clive had nothing to be worried about. Nothing to be ashamed of. Clive wouldn't do this. No reason for it whatsoever. Clive was good. Clive was their dad.'

There were more sniffles from the two younger people, and Bernard pulled them in close.

'Was Clive out last night?' asked Hope.

'Yes. I think he was going out to a pub,' said Alexis. 'I think he might have been meeting someone. He didn't say who. But he was dressed to go out.'

'He didn't say to me either,' said Bernard. 'Didn't have to. He was a grown man. Sometimes, he'd tell me who he was meeting. Sometimes not. Maybe he was off to see a friend. He said he'd be late back though, so I didn't wait up. Kids didn't wait up for him either.'

Hope saw Stephen looking at her, his eyes piercing. The kid was clearly sad. She wondered if there was more to it. Macleod always read these situations better. He told her when she'd become a detective inspector, she'd need somebody who could do what she couldn't do. She had skills he didn't have. Not just the media. Boy, did he hate the media. She would have liked to have him here right now. He'd have summed the family up, told you if anyone was hiding anything. That's what he was good at, seeing through people. Always. She was better with the evidence.

'Did he drive last night?' she asked.

'He was getting the bus,' said Bernard. 'I'd offered to drive him to wherever he wanted to go, but he said no. He was going to have a drink, so he couldn't take the car.'

110

'Did any of you hear from him after that?'

'No,' said Bernard. The kids shook their heads too.

'No phone calls,' said Hope. 'No text messages.' No, came the reply from them all. 'I take it you have a similar system to the Tilburys. You just need a card to get into the barns.'

'I thought I heard something. That's why I got up. That's why I went out,' said Bernard. 'I sleep with the window open and I thought I heard the chickens. I went to see Clive, but Clive wasn't there. He'd maybe gone to sit out by the barns. That's what I thought. Maybe he had heard something. Maybe he was out protecting them.

'I got to the last barn, the one on the edge, and I could hear the chickens, and something was up. When I went in, the light was on, but then, I struggled to see. I can't really pick out the length of the barn. The light was so bright, I switched it off and walked down with a torch. It was then that, well, that's when I found him.'

Alexis burst into tears, but Stephen remained sullen, staring ahead of him.

'You cut him down,' said Hope. 'That's what I heard in the report I received.'

'I couldn't untie it. They had pulled it tight, so I cut him down, and then I lay with him while I awaited you coming. Ambulance crew said he was gone.'

Hope turned to the liaison officer and thanked Bernard, Alexis, and Stephen for talking to her. She said she'd be back at some point soon, but made her way out of the building, keen for the fresh air of the morning. She rang Ross.

'Ross here. What's up?'

'Don't come in. Don't come up to the farm. I'm here. I can see Jona's wagon is here. Let Cunningham come up to do this and get hold of Perry. I want the two of you to go to the bus company. Clive Daniels went out on the bus last night, heading for somewhere. Check the routes towards the pub. Check the routes that leave by the farm. See if we can find him on any of the buses. Phone the landlord down at the Drowsy Duck as well, in case he was down there. We don't know where he went. Didn't say who he was going to see. That's our first port of call to find that out. I'm going to go up and see Jona. There's no point in everybody piling out here. He never committed suicide.'

'Okay,' said Ross. 'I will do. Has he been called, Perry?'

'I don't know if he's on the list. I told the desk sergeant to call the list. Give him a call, and get that list sorted for me,' said Hope.

After she closed the call, she thought that should have been Ross's job, anyway. Ross should pick up the personnel. The basics, the simple stuff. Not her. She was the boss now. She needed to become a Macleod.

No, she didn't. She needed to become Hope. Had to know what she needed covered off. What people could do for her. What they should do without asking. Like the cup of coffee Ross used to bring Macleod. They needed to understand her, what she wanted, her demands.

She walked off across the farm, taking instructions from one of the local uniformed officers to where the scene of the crime was. Arriving up close, she saw a familiar Asian woman decked out in her forensic coverall.

'I don't have a lot for you. I've only just been in.'

'Appreciate that, Jona, but I'm only looking for the initial rundown,' said Hope.

'Well, quite simple, really. They found him hanging from a

rope that was suspended over a beam at the top and tied down to a beam at the far side. Somebody put him up there.'

'What? Are you sure?'

'He was dead before he went up there. It's pretty amateur. His hands were tied behind his back at some point, and then they were cut free. You can see the marks around the wrists, but more than that, the arms have stayed in that position. They haven't come hanging fully forward. The angle of the neck is also wrong. Everything about this says that's a body that was put up there. Not suicide.

'Also pretty difficult to commit suicide like that. There was no way to get up and put yourself in the noose. Therefore, you'd had to have the noose around you and be pulling the rope to lift yourself up. That's difficult,' said Jona.

'Was it meant to look like suicide?'

'I think so. I really do.'

'Any ideas about entry? They would have had to drag him into there, wouldn't they?'

'I'm checking for footprints. Lots of people walk round here, though. Plenty of boot marks. Chickens walking all over the place. When Mr Daniels senior has come in, chickens have run everywhere as well. This is not a magnificent site to try to deal with. I need to get the chickens out first. I've walked in amongst them just to get a quick look and get some photographs before anything else gets destroyed. That's probably the clever bit. I don't know if I'm going to trace them unless there's something on the body. Perpetrator was clever in that sense.

'Okay,' said Hope. 'Keep me updated.'

She turned and walked back down towards the farmhouse, awaiting Susan Cunningham. As she approached it, she saw to the side a small figure. It was a young man in a jacket. He was dressed in black, top and bottom, his hood up, staring off into the distance. Hope walked round a little to see if she could identify him, then realised it was Stephen Daniels. He'd come outside. He turned and looked at her.

'Are you okay?' she asked. 'Can I help with anything?'

He simply stared, sullen as anything. Was he thinking something behind that? Hope wondered. He didn't look like somebody who was simply bereaved, or in shock. He seemed to be mulling over something. Hope wondered what it was.

Chapter 14

'Are you done?' asked Ross as Perry walked back into the office.

'I just needed a puff to get through,' said Perry. 'Yes, I'm good. What we got then?'

'I've pulled all the files so we can start having a good look at it,' said Ross. 'Everything's through from the bus company. There's lots of footage, so we best get on with it. You take that station over there, start going through them. I'll work through this load of files.'

Ross had secured the video playback that had been recorded on the buses. He'd given a section over to Perry, leaving the data storage unit on his desk. He'd connected it up to his computer already. All the man had to do was start looking through the files.

Ross was already through some of his and he noted down what each video was on a table showing how far away from the Daniels's Farm he would have been. Ross noticed Perry sat down, switched on the computer, brought up the first video, looked through about three seconds, and then stopped it. The man got up, scratched his backside, walked off back out of the office. When he returned five minutes later, Ross asked him,

'Where have you been?'

'Needed a wee,' said Perry.

'You couldn't have done that when you were out having a fag?'

'Didn't need one then? Needed it now. Must be getting older. Not afflict you yet, does it?' Perry sat back down again.

'Just hurry and get through those.'

'Yes, Sarge.' Perry was sitting down for another five minutes, then he was back up over towards the coffee machine. He poured himself one, brought it back over and sat down at the computer again. Ross looked at his own empty cup.

'You didn't think to get me one, did you?'

'I thought you'd be too absorbed. Sorry, Sarge, I'll get you one now.'

The way Perry said 'Sarge' made it sound like he was talking to a child, like he would tell the captain of a ship, 'Aye, aye, Captain.' There was a forced cheeriness put into the Sarge. It constantly seemed to catch Ross unawares. He glared at Perry. The man simply stood up, grabbed Ross's mug, took it over, poured him a cup and put it back on the table. Perry sat down again. As he looked through the files, he fidgeted constantly.

'Would you just get on with looking at them?'

'I am,' said Perry. 'Not my strong point, computers. Much better with talking to people. I like to be out in the field. Don't normally do this sort of work. Don't normally—'

'Go downstairs,' said Ross. 'Talk to the desk sergeant. Tell him I'd like Constable Davidson with me, please.'

Perry disappeared downstairs and Ross got on, racing through the bus videos, looking to see when Clive would get on. He quickly identified him leaving in the early evening. The image on the screen clearly matched a photograph that had been gathered from the house. Ross continued with that bus video, following it until he realised Clive had got off again. He looked at the stop. It was beside a local wood.

Ross looked for the buses that went past that stop and searched through them, racing through the videos, looking for the man getting back on. Before he got anywhere with it, Perry walked back into the room with a uniformed constable. She was in her early twenties, tall, blonde, and of the athletic build. Perry was chatting away to her, but she gave Ross a nod and sat down beside the computer screen.

'Davidson, I want you to run through the bus videos. We're looking for this man. Give Detective Perry a hand looking through those, please.'

Ross sat back down to look at his video and then turned to Perry. 'Get Constable Davidson a coffee.'

'Of course, Sarge,' said Perry.

Ross thought it might have wound the man up getting the coffee, but it wound Ross up more as he watched Perry pouring the coffee and casting glances over at Davidson. Davidson had helped previously in investigations working on the periphery. She knew how to handle the computers. Ross thought it was better that she be here keeping Perry's attention rather than Perry fumbling through the videos.

'Perry, look at this,' said Ross. He played back where Clive had got on the bus. 'I'm running through the other buses that go past there, seeing if he's come back on.'

'Good idea,' said Perry. Perry went and sat back down with Davidson as they ran through the videos that Ross had given them and Ross settled down into his work. He could go quickly, move along it easily when he wanted to. He was finding his move up to sergeant to differ from what he had imagined.

Previously, out of the team, Ross was the bottom rung. He was the one that held everything together. He was up as a DS now having to look after other people, and yet he still felt as if he was bringing in all the details, holding it all together.

There he was. Ross clocked Clive getting back on a bus and looked at the time stamp. It was two hours later, and the bus was heading back to his home.

'Can you cut out the image of that?' said Perry suddenly over Ross's shoulder.

'The image? What do you mean?'

'Get a close-up image of his face. Give me a replay of what's happening with him. I want to see him walking on, and I want to see him walking off.'

'Why?' asked Ross. 'We've clocked where he is.'

'We've clocked where he is. I want to clock what state he's in,' said Perry.

'From these images, from a bus cam.'

'It is. Indulge me, please, Sarge,' said Perry. 'You've got Davidson there. She's going through all of that stuff much quicker than me.'

Ross couldn't deny that. One thing Perry wasn't was quick around the computer. Ross printed off several images of Clive Daniels getting onto the bus, then getting off. Then he clipped the video and handed it all to Perry, several sheets of paper and a small USB stick.

Perry walked round to his own laptop, taking it out of a bag beside his desk. He left Davidson working on the main desktop. Ross watched Perry flip open the laptop, plug in the USB, and then sit there, staring at the printed paper Ross had given him with the photographs. He looked at the screen, back and forward, back and forward. He was there for a good ten minutes, Ross wondering what he was doing.

Ross was having difficulty focusing on his own job. After all, that's what he used to do. 'Do this task with that,' so Ross got on with it. Now he was tasking other people and having to look at what they were doing, and more to the point, Perry. Davidson, he knew. She'd been up before. She was good. Tell her what to do. She did it. She handed it back to him. Ross liked people to work like that. A well-oiled machine, just got on with it, just did what they were told, so he knew what was coming back. Perry was different. He was asking to do things.

Ross nearly jumped when Perry suddenly stood up. 'Have you got something?' asked Ross.

'Yes,' said Perry. 'I'll be back in a couple of minutes.'

'Where are you going?'

'I need to think.'

'Are you off for a cigarette?'

'Yes, Sarge, I said to you. I need to think.'

Ross watched Perry leave the office and wondered for a moment what was the deal with the man. He's jumping here, there, and wherever. If he'd got something, he should bring it to Ross straight away.

Ross stood up at the computer and turned to Davidson. 'Just keep going with that, okay? We've got him leaving and we've got him coming back. The route near the wood towards his house, let's look at following it on the route map, work out where he's gone next. I've tabulated where all the videos have come from, what buses, what time. It's all on that spreadsheet over there,' said Ross, pointing at a file. 'Trace it through for me, will you?'

'Of course, Ross,' said Davidson.

'I'll be back in a minute, just going to see where my esteemed colleague has got to.'

Ross marched off, happy that Davidson would do her work. He reached the outer corridor from the office, but rather than go down the stairs, which he knew Perry would have to do if he was going for a cigarette, he walked across to one of the windows.

He was up a couple of floors and could see the car park, where there was a designated smoking zone. These days very few people used it, but there was Perry. There were two other people there, constables having a chat. Perry wasn't talking to them. Instead, he was standing with one hand in a pocket, the jacket and tie on. He just looked sloppy.

Ross wore a shirt and tie, smart as always, but he thought about Macleod. He never wore fashionable ties, an older sort of gentleman's outfit. Quite drab, and he could be spruced up a lot more. The ties were dull, usually quite plain, but he looked smart.

Perry's jacket looked as if it hadn't seen a dry cleaner's in years. His shirt wasn't really ironed, and the tie—the tie looked like the knot had been done by a boy going to secondary school for the first time.

Ross watched as the first cigarette was finished, put it in the bin beside Perry, and then another was lit up. Ross picked up his phone and sent a text message down to Perry telling him that Ross was keen to hear what he'd come up with. He watched as the man pulled out his phone, looked at the message, closed the phone and put it back in his pocket. He continued with the cigarette, occasionally staring off into the distance.

It was another five minutes before the cigarette was put out and Perry started back towards the building. Ross returned to the office. When Perry came in, Ross looked up expectantly.

'What have you got for me?'

Perry looked thoughtful, then he reached down and picked up the images Ross had given him. He turned to an empty table, spreading them out on it. He then lifted the laptop across and called Ross over.

'Davidson, you want to come and look at this as well?'

Davidson could sense the tension, and she looked a little nervous as she came across to stand, just slightly aloof to the two detectives.

'Well, then, Perry, what have you got?'

'Clive's on the bus there. Look at him. What do you notice about him?'

'What do you mean,' asked Ross? 'He gets on the bus; he pays for a ticket.'

'With cash,' said Perry, 'so you can't trace him.'

'No, but the bus can.'

'Yes, but he's not hiding from us, so to speak. Why would he? Instead, he's hiding from the family. It will not be in his bank statements. Maybe somebody else sees him. Somebody else has got access to him, so he's paying with cash.'

'Or maybe it's not that far and doesn't cost that much,' said Ross. 'It's a bit of a leap.'

'It's not a leap. I'm backpedalling, sorry. Look at him. He's a cheerful man, an excited man, a man who's going somewhere.'

Ross stared at the image. 'How do you get that?'

'The way he walks, jumped onto the bus, practically. There's a definite slight excitement there, but he's also trying not to be too noticeable. Look at him when he comes back on. There's a different sort of happiness in his face, more contented, more "been and done that". The walk too. There's not a nervous excitement. He's like a man who's achieved something. A man who's—'

'Interesting,' said Davidson.

Ross glared over. He couldn't see it.

'If you now look at where he is, he's in the woods. That bus stop is by the woods. What is there around there? Where on earth does he go? What do you go to achieve in the woods? It's dark. Is he going to make a transaction? Why would you meet there? Can't be going to see somebody that he's worried about because it's in the middle of nowhere and he's not carrying any weapon. But he goes with a nervous excitement and he comes away with satisfaction. He's been seeing a woman.'

'What?' blurted Ross.

'He's being seeing a woman, and it's on the sly. More than that, they've got it together.'

'What do you mean, they've got it together?'

'They've had sex,' said Perry.

'Are you obsessed?'

'What?'

'Are you obsessed? Does everything have to involve a woman?'

'No,' said Perry. 'Oh, they're a delightful part of life.' He turned and grinned at Davidson. She gave a giggle back, but then she saw Ross's face.

'Davidson, go back and work on those videos, please. Perry, come with me,' said Ross. He marched off to the far end of the office.

'This is an investigation,' said Ross, 'A serious one, two men dead, and you're sitting telling me you're looking for sexual exploits all the time?'

'Not all the time, just following the trail, looking at the people involved, following the trail.'

'Conjecture, looking at people, that's all this is. I need evidence,' said Ross. 'I want it now, and I want your mind back out of the gutter because that's where it seems to have been since you got here. From all the quips about going to see the women at the farm, the way you look, the way you—'

'Trust me,' said Perry. 'That's a man there,' he said, pointing back towards the table with the pictures. 'He's been out, had sex, and come away again. The question is with who and why out there? Why is he now dead because of it?'

'He could be dead for several reasons,' said Ross.

Perry shook his head. 'No, the women are at the heart of this. Trust me, it'll be the women.'

'You should get on with your work,' said Ross. 'Find me some concrete evidence.' Perry shook his shoulders and walked back towards his desk with Ross shaking his head. He'd have to speak to Hope again about him. Perry couldn't stay. This was getting ridiculous.

Chapter 15

Hope was in her office, awaiting the rest of the team. She thought they were like the sea. With the tide they went out, then the team rolled back in again, looking to see what would be washed up on the beach of ideas.

She stopped for a moment. She was staring out of the window at the view Macleod loved. *Did it do this to you? Did you become more circumspect? Was it the fact you had more time on your hands, the fact you weren't out running around but sending others?*

Hope didn't think like this. Hope went out, and Hope got the details that she needed. She investigated. She worked hard. It was certainly different being the inspector, especially when the case was your own, and you weren't simply in with the DCI on a bigger case.

The first person to knock on the door was Susan Cunningham. She came in with a broad smile and a cup of coffee in her hand. When she looked outside of her office, Hope could see that Perry was pouring coffee. The next in the door was Macleod. The man looked a little hassled to Hope, but he gave her a smile and sat down at the table in the corner. Perry came through with some coffee, placing mugs down for everyone.

Soon, they were all sitting, including Jona. She seemed eager for the meeting to get going.

'Okay,' said Hope. 'This is a quick round-robin to work out where we are. First off, Jona. Regarding Roy Tilbury—can we confirm Roy is the body in the barn?'

'Yes, I can,' said Jona. 'We have dental records and they gave us a match. We're still of the belief that he was incapacitated in some way, and that's why he couldn't get out. Clearly, he wasn't dead. All facts point to his not being already deceased.'

'That ties in with the chickens being extremely restless,' said Hope. 'Any signs of anyone else, though?'

'Not that we've found so far,' said Jona. 'We'll keep working on it.'

'Staying on Roy then,' said Hope, 'Susan, what have you got for us?'

'I searched Roy Tilbury's room at the farmhouse and found a doctor's appointment. It didn't give a time; it was only a note saying doctor's appointment. Didn't say for who, but it was on a piece of paper that was stuffed way down at the bottom of a load of books in a drawer of a desk that he used for his private affairs. I acquired the details of the surgery that Roy uses, and they didn't have an appointment for him. The last one was over a year ago. I checked the other local surgeries and also checked at Raigmore. There's no appointment for Roy.'

Raigmore was the local hospital which served Inverness.

'I also observed Esme talking agitatedly to her daughter, Jenna. Her daughter said that Roy was not himself. Something was up with him but she didn't know what. When I spoke to Esme, she said that Roy was fine, actually in good spirits. Said he hadn't been near a doctor. Something's being hidden here, but I'm not sure what.'

'Susan,' said Hope, 'I think the next thing to do is for you and me to speak to Jenna. We need to push this line of enquiry. We've got two dead men. Two dead men from the egg farms, both of a similar age. Somebody's clearly hiding something over there. It doesn't sound like it's Jenna. More like she's realising something's not right. Maybe we'll need to put some pressure on Esme as well. We'll do that together.'

Susan Cunningham gave a smile, picked up her coffee and drank deeply. She was coming on well, thought Hope. Her observations and her reasoning were good. She was becoming a sound part of the team. Macleod had picked well when he grabbed her, despite all the rumours on the station.

Hope looked across towards Perry, but she couldn't see it with him. Where was Macleod coming from? Hope had been desperate, needing another detective on the case. Macleod had thrown him in. He hadn't insisted on stepping down. He hadn't insisted on coming and covering like he had done on other cases. Hope wondered what he was up to.

Hope needed to follow her lines of enquiry, so the next person she would ask about was Clive. She turned again to Jona.

'Jona. What do we know about Clive Daniels?'

'Clive Daniels was murdered. He definitely didn't commit suicide. Couldn't have pulled himself up there with a rope. So, someone put him up there. He was dead when he went up, though. Killed elsewhere and we think he was strangled.'

'There was an attempt to make it look like suicide?'

'That's right, Hope, but a terrible one. Rigor Mortis had set in, so his hands were pointed behind him, not hanging out in front. The neck had gone stiff too, meaning the angle he was hanging at was a bizarre one from what I can gather from the

126

witnesses. Of course, we didn't see him hanging there.

'The scene is an absolute mess. There's chicken poo everywhere. I've had chickens running around and trying to find anything is a nightmare. It's the proverbial needle in the chicken shit-covered haystack. I know there are some days you look at me and you think, "I wouldn't want her job." Trust me, today's that day. I'm not enjoying this one.'

'What's the likelihood of getting anything?' asked Macleod.

'There's not much on the body. Although it was dropped into the arms of his father, the father was lying down amongst all the chicken poo. Everything's heavily contaminated. We're working through it, but it's going to take time.'

'Okay,' said Hope. 'Anything else?'

'Only thing I've got is that his hands were bound at some point, we believe with a plastic tie. I've got some dimensions. It was pretty tight, but it looks like one of those standard onetime plastic ties. It might have been taken off not long after they killed him because his arms weren't in the position that they would have been with the tie in place.'

'Pretty common though, are they?'

'You could search the farms for them. We might be able to say what matches. Of course, there's no guarantee it was the farm items used. Fairly common. Sorry, not much else to go on at the moment.'

'Have we got anything else regarding Clive? Have you got anything, Ross?' asked Hope.

'We've gone through the CCTV on the buses. I've got Clive Daniels leaving his home, early part of the evening. He gets off at a wooded area. Not that far away, but far enough away from everything else to be secluded. He's back on two hours later and heads off. We're trying to trace his movements from that bus.'

'We know he went out to these woods. We know he got back on a bus, but we don't know where he went after that. That's the long and the short of it,' proposed Hope.

'Basically,' said Ross.

'Actually, there's more than that,' said Perry.

'Don't!' said Ross. 'You don't need to trouble the meeting with that.'

'I think I do,' said Perry. 'He's had sex while he's in the woods.'

'He's what?' said Hope.

'Clive Daniels had sex while he was in the woods. He's gone there to meet someone and to have sex,' said Perry.

Hope looked at Ross's face. It was like thunder.

'This is a theory produced by Detective Perry,' said Ross, 'not me.'

'How have you come by this?' asked Hope.

'Don't ask,' said Ross.

'He's definitely gone and had sex. Having been out to the Brodie farm and seeing Clive on the bus, it's quite clear he's been having sex.'

Ross was shaking his head. His hand was opening and closing into a fist.

'Are you sure this isn't just a whimsy?' asked Hope.

'It's quite clear he liked a lot of the women involved in the case,' said Perry. Ross went to stand up.

'Stop,' said Macleod. 'I can see that Ross is angry. I can see that the situation's about to get very heated. Knowing Perry from before, he will not back down from this. Maybe we can ask him to explain, *in detail*, where he's coming from.'

Hope took a step back. It wasn't like Macleod to step in that fashion. 'Okay,' said Hope. 'Lay it on us, Perry. Let us know.'

Perry stood up, disappeared out of the office for a moment, and came back in, throwing the photographs of Clive on the bus down on the table. He lined them up with before and after pictures. Then he grabbed his USB stick, giving it to Susan Cunningham, and asking her to make it come up on the screen.

'Look at the face before,' said Perry. 'That's a man who's excited. That's a man who's tense, looking to go somewhere. It's not a case of simple happiness. It's someone who's about to get a release of tension. Something's about to happen he's been looking forward to, but also worried about. The next time he gets on the bus, that's a face of a man who's satisfied,' said Perry, choosing his words carefully.

'Yet he's not just brimming, not just dancing. He's still got other cares. He's still got other worries. Something's lifted him greatly. It's been a woman. The colour on his cheeks, the way he walks. If you then tie that up with the way the women are, and I mean the younger women—'

'The younger women? He's nearly twice their age. One of the younger women's his sister. You can't be serious,' said Ross.

'Very serious,' said Perry. 'I've also spoken to the security guard, Joel. He confirmed my suspicions about the women. Several of them want the attention.'

'It doesn't mean they should get it,' said Ross.

'No, it doesn't,' said Perry. 'I'm not here to justify anyone's actions. I'm here to identify them. That man there,' he pointed at a picture of Clive Daniels, 'has been in those woods, and he's been copulating with someone. He stepped back on the bus and headed off somewhere else. We need to get down to those woods quick.'

Hope was in two minds. It seemed to be a flight of fancy. It was all conjecture; there was no hard evidence. At the end of the day, yes, they needed to go down to the woods, but where? It was an extensive area. Daniels was off the bus for quite a bit of time.

'If I may,' Macleod said to Hope, 'I think we need to follow this line as well. We need to get to where he wanted to go. It's the line we need to follow. Can I suggest, Hope, that Ross and Perry get all the bus footage from buses going into that area from time before and time after? See if we can find anybody else on them we recognise. We also should get down to the woods.'

'We should get down to the woods, whatever,' said Hope. 'He's come off there. He's been there. Maybe we can find something to back up this idea of Perry's.' Hope said the word idea as if it was the wildest shot in the dark.

'I'll be with you, Susan,' said Hope. 'Ross, Perry, buses and woods. Be quick on it. That's it, everyone.'

Hope stood up and walked back to her desk, which was usually the signal for everyone to leave. She heard them all going but felt that someone was still there. The door closed, but when she turned round, Macleod was still sitting at the table.

'Ross is annoyed at him,' said Macleod.

'It's some statement though, isn't it?'

'Why do you think he's here?' Macleod asked. 'I chose him. He didn't get picked up by anybody. I chose him. If Clarissa had said what he'd said, you'd have investigated it. You'd have followed it through. Most of policing is not about gut instinct, and yet sometimes, it is. Perry, he's a man that knows people.'

'Perry's a dinosaur, more so than you. He's like a throwback to a seventies cop.'

'Lazy, slovenly. He likes to smoke; he likes his women; he

likes women to be women, as he would say. Not the most modern sort of man, although he can appreciate them. I think that's what his words were.' Macleod laughed.

'Back in the day, you could say those sorts of things. Nowadays, you can't. He needs brought back into the modern-day fold.'

'I'll agree with that,' said Macleod. 'You can't change the way he views the world, as that's his opinion, and that's up to him. He can, however, be educated how to behave in it. He's not ridiculous in his behaviour, but it could do with being sorted. That's one of your jobs. The other job is to get the best out of him,' said Macleod.

'Ross is working with him,' continued Macleod, 'and Ross is a by-the-book, numbers man, who goes into evidence and pulls in hard physical evidence from here, there, and everywhere. Ross is a man who looks for coincidences. Perry isn't. Perry sees the people. I said you wanted someone to give you what I gave to the investigation because it's not something you have. You give a lot that's so good. That's why I had you in my team, because you covered off those things that I didn't have.'

'Are you saying Perry is you?'

'No,' said Macleod. 'He's slightly different again, but he gives you that other side. The side that doesn't sit and go through the evidence by the book. He doesn't go through on the straight-line approach. He'll give you the understanding of people.'

'Well, I've gone with Perry's approach,' she said.

'At my behest. You would have followed Ross on this one and thrown him out. Treat everybody equally. Perry's idea is good.'

'Is he right though?'

Macleod stood up and walked over to the door. 'That's for

you to find out,' he said. 'I know what I think, but I won't prejudice the investigation. You're running it. Decide. If he's got an idea, is it worth following, and then is it right?'

Macleod turned, opened the door and walked out, leaving Hope standing. She glanced out to the team in the office beyond. *Buses and woods*, she thought. *Buses and woods. Let's see if he's right.*

Chapter 16

Ross watched as Hope and Susan Cunningham left the office, going to speak to Jenna Tilbury. Perry disappeared out for a cigarette, as was becoming too much of a custom for Ross's liking. Left behind, Ross phoned the bus company, seeking more CCTV. As he was on the phone, a member of the uniformed staff arrived in the office to see only Ross and Davidson there. Ross waved them over.

'Just hold on a minute,' Ross said to the bus manager.

'I'm sorry to bother you. We've got a Peppa Brodie downstairs. She's looking to speak to someone investigating the Clive Daniels murder.'

'Fine. Thank you,' said Ross. He reached into his pocket for his mobile phone and texted a message down to Perry to pick the woman up. He said he would join them shortly, down in an interview room. Ross finished his conversation with the bus company manager, asking for a lot more CCTV and for it to be sent through to Davidson. When he closed down the call, he walked downstairs, looking along the interview rooms until he found Perry sitting inside one with Peppa Brodie.

'Sorry to have kept you,' said Ross as he entered. 'I'm here now. Can I ask what this is about?'

'It's about Clive,' said Peppa. There were tears in the woman's eyes. 'I'm afraid I have to admit to seeing him last night.'

'Seeing him?' said Ross. 'Whereabouts?'

'It was at the pub. I can't believe that they found him like that. He was fine when he left me. He was in a good mood.'

'So, you met each other at the pub? Were you in the habit of doing that?' asked Ross.

'Very much. We shared a meal. It was hoped that Clive and I would eventually get married.'

'How long have you been seeing each other?' Perry asked.

'Three months,' said Peppa. She leaned forward, tears flowing from her eyes. Ross reached inside his pocket, pulling out a clean tissue and handing it over to her.

'We're going to have to ask you some more questions,' said Ross. 'I'm sorry to put you through this, but thank you for coming forward. Which pub was it?'

'Oh, not The Duck. We wanted to, well, not keep it secret, but we were keeping it between ourselves. I mean, you can go to the pub. It's Anderson's. It's more of a restaurant, really.'

'I know it,' said Ross. 'We'll check with the manager. He would remember the both of you, would he?'

'Serving staff certainly should.'

We've got an image of what Clive was wearing, thought Ross, satisfied the staff could confirm this tale.

'You usually meet in the pub,' asked Perry, 'away from everyone else? Why was it an expectation you would get married?'

'Clive was doing well. So was I. We're of that age, aren't we? We both understand the lifestyle, farming. We wouldn't demand that much of each other beyond it. Some people can get difficult about farming. You're up early. Animals must be

134

taken care of. Some wives don't understand that. Some men don't either, just easy between us. Then we could also combine the farms. Clive was doing so well with his farm, truly up and coming. Could have helped with ours as well.'

'Was it more of a business transaction then?'

'No, no,' said Peppa, wiping her eyes. 'Not at all. We liked to meet and talk. It's hard being in the middle. You've got the older ones who want to tell you how to do everything and the younger ones who tell you that you're too old for anything. I was past it, according to my kids. Nobody was going to want to settle down with someone like me, especially with my mother looking on. I'm not like her. I'm a lot more convivial. She's on her own because of how she is. I was just an unfortunate accident.'

'Okay,' said Ross. 'How long did you have your meal for?'

'A couple of hours and then he headed off again.'

'You say you were keeping it quiet from others,' said Ross. 'Clive was of that opinion as well?'

'We never said where we were going to anyone, but it was always that pub. I thought I should come forward because nobody else will say we were meeting. But that's what it was why, and that's what we were doing. It's all gone now though,' she said. 'We didn't leave together, by the way. As I say, we were keeping it quiet. Therefore, he came on the bus and I came in my car.'

Perry was clearly itching to ask something. He looked across at Ross twice. It appeared to Ross that Perry almost shrugged his shoulders and then blurted out the next question.

'Were you having sex?' asked Perry.

Ross flicked his head round. 'What?'

'I said, were they having sex? Just establishing the degree of the relationship.'

'Well,' said Peppa, 'no, we haven't got to that stage yet. The kids call it "made out", don't they? Kissed a few times outside the pub before we left each other.'

'Did you make out this time?'

'No, I was still inside when he left.'

'Okay.' said Perry. 'What instigated this?'

'I'm sorry?'

'What instigated your relationship together? How did you come to start it? Who said let's go for a meal?'

'I knew Clive had been looking at me for a while. He was getting to that age. I was at that age, but he was a very reserved man, heavily engrossed in the business. Outside of that, he wasn't particularly good with people, so I asked him, said let's go for a meal. Let's talk, and it went from there.'

'How do you think your families would feel about the two of you together?' asked Ross.

'My mother, she'd probably be okay with it if it brought the chicken farms together. The girls don't give a toss about what I do. Too busy with themselves, thinking they look like superstars. Dressed up to grab your man's attention. Did with him, didn't they?' she said, pointing to Perry. 'You were a lot more dispassionate. Didn't seem to influence you at all.'

'They're not my type,' said Ross. 'What about on the other side? Did Clive ever talk about that?'

'I can't see that Mr Daniels would be bothered. Bernard's an old man now. Clive was practically running everything, anyway. I don't know what he'll do now. You've got Alexis and you've got Stephen. I don't know if Alexis will want to run the place and Stephen's still very young. It's left Bernard in a real quandary, and he's lost his son. We've lost—.'

Peppa broke down again. Ross took a moment, then waved down a uniformed constable, asking her to sit with Peppa while he had a discussion with Perry outside.

'Do you mind if we take this outside? I can get a cigarette in,' asked Perry.

'I damn well do,' said Ross. 'Were you having sex? He's just died, for goodness' sake. "Were you intimate?" is the phrase.'

'Okay, fancy word, intimate. I wanted to be clear. Sex is sex, isn't it?'

Ross raised his eyebrows at him. 'You've got to understand the person you're interviewing.'

'That you do,' said Perry. 'Came forward to clear her name, offer any assistance.'

'She's quite distraught,' said Ross.

'That she is, and it's about the only thing that's making me think there was any sort of relationship here. What man goes, has sex with somebody, and then pops along to talk to someone else about being married to them? He's got to have some sort of a kink, or else we're not seeing this correctly.'

'What do you mean we're not seeing this correctly?'

'I'm not sure,' said Perry. 'Usually, I have a cigarette and have a think about it.'

'Have a thinking in here without clogging up your lungs,' said Ross. 'She's come forward, talking about eventually getting married. It all makes sense, putting the farms together.'

'If the farms wanted to go together,' said Perry, 'then why not? Look at them, they're both in their forties. You would have been talking to them in their twenties. You'd have been arranging it then. They could have pulled the farms together at that time. As I understand it, supermarkets are looking for bigger and bigger suppliers, not little individual ones. It would have benefited them all round. Something isn't right here.'

'We go back in there,' said Ross. 'I want you to show a bit more decorum and respect.'

'Yes, Sarge. What are we going to ask her?'

'Ask her for a bit more detail about him. See if they really had a relationship. We'll check if she had a meal with him regularly.'

'That's not a relationship,' said Perry, 'knowing that somebody has meals together.'

'It's meals together on the quiet.'

'But it takes two to have a relationship,' said Perry. 'Why are they there? Could be business discussions, could be anything else, doesn't have to be a relationship. They could have had an issue in the past. She could be covering here by coming in. Just because she's come in doesn't mean it's actually a good thing. It doesn't mean that she's owning up out of the goodness of her heart. She could be trying to cover up.'

'This was their social circle,' said Ross. 'Stands to reason they find each other within it.'

'Stands to reason they could find each other for many reasons, not necessarily to do with—they're in their forties. You get together at that stage, then you want to know the penny fits the slot early, don't you?'

'Would you get your mind out of the gutter?' said Ross. 'Not everybody just jumps into bed.'

'That's the thing. We want to think the best of everybody. Don't do that. Think the worst. Look at them from the other side and then prove it wrong. Then you find more and more holes in the cheese and you suddenly realise how people are.'

'What?' blurted Ross. 'No, we dig out the evidence. The evidence at the moment says they're having an enjoyable meal together. We'll go talk to the owner of the pub.'

'Go on then,' said Perry. 'Talk to him right now before we go in, so we know what we're going to say.'

'What are you going to do? Keep her company?' asked Ross.

'I'm going for a fag and a think,' said Perry.

Ross disappeared back upstairs, found the phone number of the pub and called, looking for the landlord. He confirmed that Peppa Brodie was there, and that she met Clive Daniels on about a weekly basis. He'd seen none of the rest of the family there, but he knew them well from being in the local area.

Ross returned downstairs and found Perry hanging around outside the interview room. As Ross got closer, he swore that the trousers and jacket smelt even more of smoke than before.

'Got any nicotine thoughts for me?'

'You think they could have been calling something off? Maybe there could have been an issue? You think she could have been sleeping with someone else?'

'What?' Ross was getting annoyed now with the conjecture that was being fired out. That was not how this murder team worked. You looked for something, you found evidence, and then you rationalised what was happening, not just come up with wild accusations.

'Maybe he's met somebody beforehand and then he's gone to meet her. The reason it hasn't got formal is he's heard something about someone else. Maybe he's heard something about her. She's not telling us.'

'Can we go in and finish the interview?' asked Ross.

'Of course. I'm just getting things in my head,' said Perry.

'You want to sort your head out,' said Ross. 'You want to give it a good clean down because the stuff it comes out with, it's like an episode of a soap.'

'You know soaps are based on reality,' said Perry. 'They're all just condensed. They're just shoved in and then hyped up a bit. That's why many people don't see it in real life. Things are like this in real life. People cheat, people mess about, but they try to keep it quiet. It's not always so dramatic. I think there's a lot less shouting, really.'

Ross was getting deeply annoyed now at Perry. He rabbited on about nonsense, about nothing that was essential to the investigation. Ross ignored him and went back into the interview room, and Perry sat down beside him a few seconds later.

'I've confirmed where you were, Peppa. Unfortunately, the landlord was at a distance, so we won't be able to confirm your link to Clive but thank you for that. When Clive arrived, how did he seem?'

'He was happy. It was our time together. He went away happy, too. We were going to make plans, make things happen on a better scale. We thought about possibly even going away.'

'Where to?' asked Perry.

'We hadn't really thought about it, trying to work out what both of us would like.'

'What did you talk about with that sort of thing?' asked Perry.

'Not much. That's why I wasn't sure. He wasn't a holiday man. He said very little.'

'What about his interests?'

'Just the chicken farms. That's why Clive did so well. That's why he was dominant in making the business succeed.'

'Thank you for coming in,' said Ross. 'It must have been a hard time.'

'It was,' said Peppa. The woman was escorted away, back

outside the station, and Ross looked at Perry.

'What do you think, then? You think she did it? Is that what's coming through from your nicotine-fuelled senses?'

'No, but she didn't have an affair with him. She wasn't starting something and she sure as heck would not go on holiday with him. The woman knows nothing about him. She was talking business. He was meeting her regularly. They were talking business. Be assured of it.'

Ross shook his head. All conjecture. They needed something real, not Perry rambling. They'd go back to the footage from the buses. Then, when they'd checked that, it would be time to see what they could find down in the woods.

Chapter 17

Susan Cunningham pulled the car up in front of the Tilburys' farmhouse and glimpsed surprise from Esme Tilbury. She was working at a plant in a pot beside the front door, but she stood up with her gardening gloves still on and a small trowel in one hand. Hope stepped out from the passenger seat and Susan turned off the car engine, following her outside the car.

'My, Inspector, what are you doing here?'

'I'm sure you've heard Clive Daniels is dead and I'm just here to ask some routine questions about people's whereabouts.'

'You don't seriously think some of us could have done it?'

'We have to look at all angles and at the moment there seems to be more connection between yourselves, the Brodies, and the Daniels as the bigger egg producers. More than just families that congregated together down at the Duck.'

'I thought you'd be looking at the animal rights lot.'

'Not a lot about this says animal rights,' said Hope. 'I keep an open mind, but animal rights protesters tell you what they've done and why they've done it. To actually kill someone as well is not their style. The thing is that people are all for animals being looked after until you go too far. You kill a human to

142

defend an animal. Most people won't back you. You'd have to be a true nutter to do that.

'Most people who are into animal rights are not nutters. They have a reasonable thought process behind what they're doing. You might agree with it; you might disagree, but they don't do stupid things like saying animals are worth more than humans and they certainly don't take lives. Not deliberately.'

'You're the detective. I'll leave that sort of thing to you,' said Esme.

'Is Jenna around?' asked Hope.

'I think she's up in her room. Why?' asked Esme.

'We want to talk to her as well. I'm sure she's been having a hard time of it, but we need to tick the box.'

'I'll get her here then,' said Esme.

'It's better if we talk to you separately,' said Hope. 'I'll talk to you. Detective Constable Cunningham here will see Jenna. I'm sure that would be fine.'

Esme looked to protest but then seemed to resign herself to the fact that Susan Cunningham was going to speak to her daughter.

'Up the stairs, along the hall, second on the right. She should be in there. Knock the door before you go in.'

As if I was just going to march in, thought Susan. *I might be a lot younger than you, but you don't have to talk to me like that.*

Susan climbed the stairs and walked along the hallway, glancing left and right. She'd been there not that long before, checking through Roy Tilbury's room. His sister's room was only across from it.

She rapped on the door and got a quiet, 'Come in.' Susan opened it, entered and closed the door behind her. Jenna was sitting on her bed gazing at her phone, but she flung it down on seeing Susan enter.

'Yes? You want something?' asked Jenna.

'I want to ask you about your brother. You've heard that Clive Daniels is dead?'

'I heard,' said Jenna. 'Talk of him committing suicide.'

'Definitely wasn't suicide. I don't know what's going on. I don't know why,' said Susan. 'I want to talk to you about your brother. Maybe shed some light on everything.'

'What do you want to know about him?'

'You're old enough. Nineteen, isn't it?' Jenna nodded. 'Your brother have any girlfriends? I know he's considerably older than you, but did he have any love interests? He's at that stage of life where he will not commit to anything unless he's sure.'

'None that I knew of,' Jenna said.

'What do you mean by that? It's a funny way to answer it. Most people would say no.'

'He had his laptop in his room, the one you've taken away. He always seemed to be on it late at night. Said he was chatting, but it was often to the same person.'

'How do you know it was the same person? Did you hear their voice?'

'No. Never. Never did he speak with the voice. It was always typing.'

'Okay,' said Susan. 'How did you know it was the same person?'

'It was a chat room. Always the same tag, opened up in a private chat.'

'What were they called, then?' asked Susan.

'Just MTB. That's all it said. MTB. No idea who that is. I've thought about it a lot. I thought about people we meet, but there's no one with those initials.'

'How long had he been speaking to this person?'

'Four months? Yes, MTB was about four months.'

'What sort of things did he say to them?'

'I don't know. I saw little of the chat because Roy would close the chat down whenever I came in. He was quick on it. I just was quicker and saw the tag he was talking to.'

'You think it was just fun?'

'He was always determined on it. He always seemed to enjoy the chat. I don't know—I think Mum caught him on it. She saw his chats, but she didn't tell me anything about it. I'm the young one, the daft one. The one that doesn't understand. I understood my brother better than her. People always said that he was about the farm, but there was more to him than that. More to him than just getting up every day and seeing how many eggs have been laid. Roy had a good sense of humour. He didn't get to exercise it much in this house, but he had a good sense of it. He used to make me laugh when I was younger.'

'Did you get on well then?'

'We did, but he was older. Roy and I, we never shared secrets or that. We're in a different time of life.'

'Was he lonely?'

'Possibly. Although, it wasn't like he was fixated on this chat. If I came in and said we're going down to the pub tonight, he'd offer to take me. He always went down with me. He said it was good for me as we were meeting all the other young people from the egg farms. Never a problem. Took me down. I guess maybe it was because he didn't have that sort of taxi service. I was somebody to come out with him. He was held back quite a bit. It's not until recently that we all started going out and meeting as young people. In the old days, it used to be all the older ones. We met as families. These days, no. We got together, and we had fun.'

'When you went down to the Drowsy Duck, what did he do?'

'He talked little. He'd sit there with his pint.'

'Clive Daniels went down often too, didn't he?'

'He did.'

'Did he talk to Clive? After all, they're more of the same age.'

'To a point. Often, they'd sit apart at the bar, drinking their own pints. I think they both just wanted out. I was down to see my friends.'

Susan went to get up. Jenna grabbed her by the hand. 'I miss him. Do you know that? I really miss him. It wasn't those animal rights people, though, was it? Animal rights people don't do that sort of thing. Somebody's come after him. Now somebody's come after Clive. If you're at that level, you must be getting worried.'

Susan walked to the door and then stopped, looking around at photographs in the room. There were some of Roy, a lot of him with Jenna. There weren't many of her mum.

'You and your mum don't get on very well, do you?'

'I was an afterthought. Maybe I was a father getting too frisky one night. Something like that. She's never wanted me. He has. She never did. Don't know why. Maybe she had a rough time having me. They say that about women sometimes. You haven't had kids, have you?'

Susan shook her head.

'Well, I know it can change women sometimes. We don't all handle them the same. At least that's what I've read. I'm too young to have kids. Difficult at this age. Roy had the right idea. Keep going on your own. He had just about everything he wanted. The trouble was, he didn't know what he really wanted. Any gadget going. Anything that was good for the computer. Roy could just buy it. Nobody could buy him anything.'

'Forgive me for asking, but if he was looking for someone, would Roy be interested in any of the Brodies?'

'Peppa, you mean?'

'No, not necessarily.'

'The other ones are young like me. Roy never looked at me in that way. I hope you're not insinuating.'

'No, I was asking about the Brodies,' said Susan. 'Just keeping a wide notion about what could have gone on. It's part of the job. I'm not meaning any offence.'

'Roy was a quiet soul, so trying to work out his taste in women would not be easy. It wasn't like I walked in here and found him on a website for women over fifty.' Jenna laughed a bit. 'I suppose actually that wouldn't have been that far off his age, would it? He'd probably be more worried if he turned round after looking at a load of teens.'

'I shouldn't have brought it up,' said Susan. 'I apologise. I just need to get a picture of him, try to understand what was going on with him. If we go back to his chats; MTB, still not ringing a bell?'

'No, I'm sorry.'

Susan nodded and left, walking down the stairs to the living room, where Hope was engaged in conversation with Esme. Esme seemed rather defensive.

'It's one thing to be jealous of each other. It's one thing to look at each other's business and think, I wish we'd do that. That's just business. We're okay, most of us. We kept going. Because of that, we're stable. Challenges always come from supermarkets and that. You ride them. We're big enough.'

'I'm just a little worried that we have two men of a similar age killed off. I need to find the links between them. We're still doing a lot of work around the barns, trying to work out who could have been in there. Why was he burned alive in a chicken house? It just seems such a waste. Crazy.'

'Animal rights,' said Esme. 'It'll be animal rights.'

Hope nodded and walked over to Susan Cunningham, who was standing politely at the door. 'Thank you for your help,' said Hope. 'Where's Donald? We'll quickly interview him as well.'

While Esme disappeared, Hope asked Susan what she'd learnt.

'Roy was having online chats with MTB. That was the caller's signature. On his laptop in chat rooms although Jenna said that he disappeared out with her quick enough to go down to the pub.'

'Maybe just a bored pastime? Did he actually know someone on there?' asked Hope. 'You got his laptop, didn't you?'

'Sitting with forensics. I'll give Jona a ring and try to direct her where to go.'

Hope and Susan interviewed Donald, finding out he'd been out on the farm last night. Hope was bothered by the casual antagonism between the farms, but couldn't put her finger on what was bothering her. Cunningham had pulled out some good details, though.

Something Jenna had said. Her brother wasn't obsessed with what was on the screen. Not when he was going to meet the other young people from the farms. The other young people and Clive as well. Peppa too. Maybe Peppa had been interested in Roy.

Together with Susan Cunningham, Hope drove back towards the station.

'What do you think of Perry?' asked Hope.

'He seems to get some people's backs up, boss,' said Susan.

'I asked you what you thought about him.'

'I get on fine. Yes, he makes the odd comment, but I was used to that downstairs. He has said nothing bad. Nothing explicit. He's not a bad person. Certainly comes in with some interesting theories.'

'Does he remind you of anyone?'

'A bit. He reminds me of the boss.'

'In what way?' asked Hope.

'He's a thinker, isn't he? More of a thinker than a doer, that's to be sure.'

'Unless he's smoking. He can do that all right.'

'You can't blame him for that. That's an addiction.'

Everybody's telling me what I can't do, thought Hope. *I'm going to push him. I'm going to push out of him what he knows. Get him to prove it. He'll either fall on his face and be out the door, or he'll prove me wrong.*

'You've got to think those things, Susan. You've got to think that if the boss brought him on board and he's worked with him, he must have seen something in him,' said Hope. 'I just wish he could tell me what it is.'

Chapter 18

Hope stepped out of the car at the station and marched over towards the steps that led to the rear entrance. As she did so, she noticed Perry was standing by the smoking area. He had a cigarette that looked about finished. He waved at her and then lit up another one.

'I need to speak to Ross and you,' shouted Hope. 'Don't light that!'

Perry gave an immense sigh before putting the cigarette back in the packet. He wandered over towards the station, stopping to talk to Susan Cunningham on the way over. From the doorway, Hope looked back at the two of them. He seemed to be quite engaged with Susan, his face lighting up.

She watched Perry. He certainly looked enthralled by the younger woman. Susan was an attractive young woman, but was Perry interested in her because of what he'd heard? Hope was finding it difficult to shake off the way she felt about Perry. He has a greasiness to him. He also seemed lazy with it. Always down for some smokes. She wondered what he'd be like chasing a suspect.

She gave them a shout and told them to hurry and then stormed up to her own office. As she passed the outer office, she told Ross to come in with the other two as soon as they got up the stairs because she wanted to know what they had.

The investigation was discovering possibly important information, but nothing conclusive. It wasn't going anywhere fast. She needed her answers, and quickly. There were two dead now. Would a third come? In her experience, if things were being covered up, more deaths often happened.

Ross marched into her office after knocking, putting his laptop down on the desk and linking it up to the screen at the side. Hope could smell Perry come in before she heard him, but he was laughing with Susan Cunningham.

'Okay, let's get serious,' said Hope, casting a glance over at the pair of them. 'What have you two got?'

'Well,' said Ross. 'We've been through the buses and the camera work. We got the arrival of Clive Daniels at the woods previously. The other thing is, though, now that we've gone on beyond that, we've found someone else.'

'Who?' asked Hope.

'Sarah Brodie. Sarah's on a bus shortly before Clive arrives. She gets off at that stop. She then gets back on a bus after Clive leaves. It's going in an opposite direction, but it's not long after Clive leaves.

'Just to get this in my head,' said Hope. 'Sarah arrives at the bus stop, gets off into the woods. Clive arrives shortly afterwards. Clive then gets back on another bus. Shortly after, Sarah gets back on.'

'There you go,' said Perry. 'They're obviously not hiding from us, the law, but they're keeping it quiet, both arriving on a bus.'

'Well, Sarah has to. She's not driving,' said Cunningham.

'Where's the image of Sarah arriving?' asked Hope.

Ross pressed a button. A slightly blurred camera image from inside the bus was shown of Sarah Brodie.

'Would you look at that,' said Perry. Hope cast her eyes over at him. 'I'm just saying, look, that's not a girl that's going out for a hike in the woods, is it?'

'She certainly isn't. You might go clubbing in that if you were somewhere warm,' said Susan.

'That's enough. Let's just keep to the facts here,' said Hope.

'Those are the facts,' said Perry. 'She's dressed, using an old expression, up to the nines, dressed to—'

'Don't use that expression,' said Hope. 'She's not dressed to kill.'

'Well, you're right there,' said Perry. 'She's dressed for sex.'

Hope looked over at him. 'We don't know that.'

'We know that the two of them are there at the same time. Then, lo-and-behold,' said Perry, 'he's off along the road, apparently talking to her mother.'

'What?'

'I was coming to that,' said Ross, 'while you were out, Peppa Brodie came in, announced that she met Clive at a pub close by. Apparently, and I've checked this out, they met regularly, starting recently, the last lot of months. She said that they were looking at getting together and going to be married.'

'She also said that she was going off on holiday with him and yet when I questioned her, she had absolutely no idea about what he liked. Didn't know any of his interests. After meeting a guy for three months, she knew sod all about him,' said Perry.

Hope was surprised. She reckoned Perry would probably think she was having sex with him as well.

'Did they meet anywhere outside of the pub? Was there any other relationship going on?' asked Hope.

'I asked her if she was having sex.'

'He put it like that,' said Ross, looking at Hope's face.

'You asked a woman who apparently was having relations, or a relationship at least, with a man who's just died if she was having sex. You could have been a bit more discreet!' barked Hope.

'I could have asked her if they were intimate, yes,' said Perry, 'but she didn't blanch at the question, you know. Did either of you ever think I might have asked it in that way for a reason?'

'Let's just chill it down a bit,' said Hope. 'It's not about us. It's not about what we are doing. There's a case in the middle of this. She turned around and said that she wasn't having sex with him.'

'That's correct. Didn't bat an eyelid,' said Perry.

'She wasn't meeting him for a relationship. What was it? A tiddlywinks competition?' said Hope.

'I think it's to do with the farms,' said Perry.

'That's conjecture. We do not know what they talked about. I talked to the landlord who confirmed him to be there,' said Ross, 'but he didn't know what they talked about.'

'Did you ask her, did she ever get lovey-dovey? Did they ever kiss?' asked Hope.

'She said they only ever did that outside the pub,' said Ross.

'Exactly,' said Perry, 'exactly. There's no evidence to prove that she was in a relationship. There's only evidence to prove that she met him on a weekly basis, away from everyone else.'

'Sounds like a relationship though, doesn't it?' said Hope.

'Sounds like. You people have just got onto me constantly about evidence. Yet when I put evidence in front of you, you're not willing to knock down what's been put up by Peppa Brodie.'

He's right, thought Hope. *He's certainly right with that.*

'Then let's focus on evidence. Susan updated me on the way back in the car. Roy Tilbury used to have chats on his laptop with somebody with the initials of MTB. This seemed to be about as intimate as Roy got with anyone. The only other place he went out to was the pub with all the younger people. Both he and Clive went. MTB didn't keep him at home. Jenna thought he was obsessed, but it never stopped him from coming out to the pub.'

'Now that's interesting,' said Perry.

'Why?' asked Hope.

'Not sure yet, but it doesn't mean he wasn't obsessed. Does it? Maybe it means—'

Perry stopped for a moment, thinking.

'Are you needing another cigarette?' spat Ross.

'That's enough,' said Hope. 'You two, out to the woods.'

Ross glared over at her. 'We are getting around to that. We've just been doing—'

'I didn't ask for an explanation. I just said right now we need to get down to those woods. We've just proved that somebody was there. Perry, we're talking evidence. We know that Sarah Brodie was there. We know Clive Daniels was there. At the moment we have a coincidence that they're in the same place. We need to prove that they met. If you're still obsessed that he had sex, we need to prove it. Get me evidence.'

'You can't be serious. She's miles younger than him,' said Ross.

'And?' said Perry. 'He's a man, a single man. He's a lonely man, a man who sees her at the Drowsy Duck regularly.'

'We don't have evidence to say that he was deeply engaged with her at the pub. Roy Tilbury's a better bet with his laptop chats.'

'Yet Clive's always there, isn't he?' said Perry.

'Susan, get on to the techies. Get into that laptop. Find out if there's any evidence of what was said. Often chats are still on them. We'll see who Roy was chatting to.'

'It could take time, though,' said Perry. 'You have to go careful with that one.'

'I am aware,' said Hope. 'Because of that, get down to those woods. See if you can find out where any of them went. See if you can prove that they met.'

Hope stood for a moment, thinking. 'What's it saying about him? If he meets Sarah Brodie.'

'If he's having sex with her, and then meets her mother, he's either got a heck of a kink,' said Perry, 'or somebody's not telling the truth. We've got the wrong end of the stick.'

'Got the end of some sort of stick, though,' said Hope.

'Right.' Perry walked forward and picked up the photograph of Sarah Brodie getting back onto the bus. He turned and held it up in front of Hope. Then in front of Susan. 'I'm happy to defer to your better knowledge here,' he said. 'I believe she's had sex.'

Hope shook her head. 'Evidence, Perry. Okay. Get me evidence. Not half-baked ideas. I know you've got a story forming in your head. You've got to prove it. Until then, keep it in your head and keep it as a possibility.'

Susan Cunningham was sitting looking at the picture now. She turned to Hope. 'He might have a point.'

Hope looked at the picture. Sarah looked like she was out clubbing, not like she was deeply distressed, moved, or enthralled. Hope didn't need this, and she certainly didn't need Susan going off with Perry's ideas.

'Susan, go sort the computer. Then get down to talk to Sarah.

I'm going to get a hold of Jona; see if she's got any evidence from the crime scenes that actually brings people into it.'

As the team were dismissed and walked out of her office, Hope saw somebody else outside. It used to be that Hope always loved to sit with Macleod and talk through cases. Sure, he could be an arse at times, but he was a clever man. Just lately it was almost like he was being a granddad. He was there ahead of her, waiting for her to catch up, and yet he wasn't even running this case.

'What?' said Macleod as she looked at him coming in.

'Are you here to show me you've got it cracked already?'

'Whoa,' he said. 'You got a problem with that lot in there, you take it out on them. I'm your boss and I'm here for an update. It's what I do. I've just had an update from Clarissa. Strangely enough, for being the rowdy and quite blunt person she is, she actually delivered the update in a much more passive and cheerful tone.'

Hope turned away and walked over to the window. 'He's bloody obnoxious,' she said.

'Really?'

'He asked a woman whose believed partner is dead, was she having sex with him? What sort of way is that to ask something?'

'Confrontational way,' said Macleod. 'I don't know if he was justified or not, but that's a confrontational way.'

'I don't think he was bloody justified.'

'That's your issue. Deal with that. It's your team now. I keep telling you that.'

'Yes, you do.'

'Yes, I do,' said Macleod, 'because you keep coming to me as if you're looking for some answers.' He lowered his voice. 'Perry is currently your DC. Whether he remains your DC is up to you. Like I said before, is he right, is he wrong? The other side of it, how he's dealing with people. That's a management issue. Sort it. Do I need to send you off on a people skills course? I thought we did that with inspectors nowadays. It wasn't like my days when you got proven by the cases you cracked. You didn't get any extra points for keeping everyone in check.'

'Perry might be right,' said Hope. 'I've sent him off to get evidence. He might be right. Clive Daniels may have got off that bus for sex. Sarah Brodie was there. That's all we know. Both there at the same time. It's the woods in the dark. She's either running drugs with him, or they're there for a bit of sex. Or there's something we're missing. The trouble is, he's then meeting Sarah's mother. Peppa's told us she's having a relationship with him as well, but without sex. Perry says she doesn't seem to know much about him. Why rush in and tell everybody you are meeting?'

'Good,' said Macleod. 'That's good. At least we're getting somewhere.'

'You think?'

'You've got a bucket of questions and they keep spilling out more questions. You know how this goes. Stop worrying about solving it and just keep asking the questions. Keep channelling your line through. You're an inspector now. You're at the top. Get your backside out there and get involved in it. Get up close.'

'Get your what?'

'Sorry,' Macleod said. 'You're frustrated; so am I. This is your team, Hope. I put somebody in to help you and you're worried about whether he's speaking correctly. The case first. Solve it first. Deal with the other stuff along the way. Is he useful for you? Yes, or no.

'Why do you think Ross was on the team for me? He was useful, covered everything off. He's up as a sergeant now. Is he still covering everything off? Is he still running everything? Should Susan be doing that? What's Susan's role?

'You were with me mostly when I was an inspector. I sent you off for the really important stuff. I brought Kirsten on back in the day because she was like me. She was good for the rest of the team, but I worked little with her. You've got to match your people up. Ross and Clarissa. Ross by the book, Clarissa not so. Match him up. Perry will bring out the best in Ross, eventually. He'll change him. He'll give him the side that he hasn't got. That's if Perry's the right person for you. That was my thinking. He'd also do it for you and give you what I was giving you. That way of looking at things. It's your team. You've got to do it. I'm just here for the updates.'

'I might not make you a coffee every time you come down.'

Macleod laughed. 'I've got somebody to make me coffee upstairs whenever I want it. I don't need Ross anymore for that. You've got to decide what you need, but understand, you've just told me Perry was right, or at least you think he was. When you were initially on the team with me, I saw a brazen woman. I saw somebody who was so different from me. I saw a distraction until I worked with you, and then I saw a brilliant young individual.

'I saw somebody who could be an inspector. Don't see that anymore.' Hope looked over at him. 'I see *the inspector*. You're not capable of being an inspector. You are one. Get rid of all the insecurities you've ever carried because you can't afford them now. This is you. Own it and own this team. Get me a killer, Hope, whether it's one or two. Get me this case solved.

No more bodies, please.'

'Is that the DCI inspirational speech?'

'It's the DCI inspirational speech I've been used to for most of my life, so yes,' said Macleod. 'I thought I did the inspirational bit just before that. No more bodies. Let's go.'

He turned and almost skipped out in a fashion that Hope wasn't used to at all. She was under the cosh and he just told her to embrace it. *Oh well,* she thought, *guess it's time to.*

Chapter 19

Susan Cunningham parked the car up in front of the Brodie house. As she did so, an older woman appeared at the door, walking out towards her. *Lorraine Brodie*, thought Susan, recognising the face from the case board they had in the station.

'Who might you be? We're busy here.'

'Detective Constable Susan Cunningham.'

'Is that all I get? I got a sergeant last time. I told him what he needed to know, and he went away. Why are you back?'

'I wish to speak to Sarah. I need to speak to her alone.'

'Sarah? You want to speak to the child?' fumed Lorraine.

'Sarah's no child in the eyes of the law. She's twenty-two, a grown woman. She's no more a child than you are,' said Susan. 'I wish to speak to her. Call her, but she can have someone with her if she wants.'

'She'd like to have me with her.'

'Why's that?' asked Susan.

'Because people twist words. She is a child, even if she is twenty-two. They all are. You don't stop looking after them. Even Peppa's still a child, in a way. Still needs me about.'

Susan could see a figure just lingering inside the doorway

of the house. 'Is that you, Sarah?' she asked. The girl stepped out. 'I need to speak to you alone. I need to ask you some questions.'

'And I can be here with you. It's not a problem,' said Lorraine. The woman's eyes were fixed on Susan.

Susan wondered what to do. Should she insist on the girl speaking? How would she get past the older woman? Should she insist she come down to the station? At the moment, it was only enquiries. Susan wasn't being forcibly brought in. That was the last thing she needed.

Susan wanted the truth. After all, Clive had been alive when he got back on the bus. He'd left before her. She'd got on a bus going in the opposite direction. It would be quite something for her to have doubled back, found him again, and then killed him. If Perry was right, why would she want to kill him? There was no good reason. Understanding what she was about and what she could do to help Susan understand Clive as a person was the key thing. Not to walk into a stalemate. Maybe she'd have to play this a different way.

'I'd like to speak to Sarah alone, as I've said.'

'And I will be with her, right here,' said Lorraine.

'I can insist she comes down to help with the enquiries. I can bring her down to the station. She'd be entitled to a lawyer. At the moment, these are only enquiries. Nobody's formally insisting on anything.'

'We're busy,' said Lorraine. 'Susan's got to muck out some of the barns. She's got things to do.'

'Well, maybe I'll come back later,' said Susan. She stared the old woman down. The woman looked back with an intensity that promised she wasn't going away. 'I'll be seeing you,' said Susan.

She stepped back inside her car, reversed it, and drove away. She drove it down the road until it was out of sight of the house and parked it up, hiding it in amongst some trees. It wasn't totally hidden away, but she doubted that any of the Brodies would leave the farm soon. Susan jumped over a fence, back into the farmyard. She crossed some fields, keeping low until she got up to where the hen barns were.

Susan stayed down low, watching the farmhouse, and sure enough, Sarah soon walked over. She wore Wellington boots and jeans, a large jacket, and her hair was tied up. A very different image from the one she'd had on the bus. Susan watched as she talked to a couple of farmhands and walked along the back of the chicken houses.

She activated one of the doors with a keycard and stepped inside. There were chickens running around outside, and Cunningham thought there was never a better time to speak to her. She was far away from the farmhouse.

Cunningham kept within the line of the hen barns, so no one further up could see her until she got close. She then walked along the barn edges. She came to the hen barn she'd seen Sarah walk into. The door wasn't open, so she rapped on it gently. The door opened, and Sarah stood looking back at her.

'You said it would be down in the station. Why?'

'I said a lot of things. Let's face it, I wasn't going to talk to you without your grandmother being there. I need to talk to you about a personal matter.'

'She won't be happy about that,' said Sarah. 'I'm not sure I want to anger her in that way.'

'You want to talk to me, Sarah. We know you were on the bus and you met Clive before he died. I need to talk to you about him. Like I said over at the farmhouse, I can do it at the station. We know you left on the bus, going the other direction. I don't think you killed him, but I need to know about him. I need to know what's going on.'

'Inside, quick,' said Sarah. She closed the door behind her. Inside the barn, the floor was covered with chicken poo. There were large feeders here and there, as well as perches leading up to where the hens would lay. The noise inside wasn't deafening, but there was certainly more than an undercurrent of clucking.

'What was the deal between you and Clive?' asked Susan.

'Clive was, well, he was good, fun, special. Maybe a ticket out of this place.'

'You were seeing him then.'

'Very much,' said Sarah. 'He used to come down to the pub, but we couldn't do anything at the Duck. I could talk to him on the quiet, whisper the odd word in his ear, but everyone else was around, so we couldn't get intimate. He'd been interested in me for several years, but he said that as a teenager, it wasn't worth the risk. He didn't know how I would react. When I was older, he felt he could talk about the way he felt.'

'Whose idea was the woods, then?' asked Susan.

'Mine. Easy to get to on the bus. My mother had also started meeting with him. Clive used it as a cover. He always came on the bus so nobody would see him, and he could see if anybody followed. I went on the bus because I have no car. I don't drive. The woods are sheltered and if the weather was too rough, we wouldn't go until we found our place. We found what was for us. He always seemed such a dull guy, down at the Duck. Boring guy at the meetings, but Clive wasn't just clever about egg farms. He was quite an excellent lover.'

'Have you had much experience?' asked Susan, trying to not make it sound like a disparaging comment.

163

'Plenty. Not that anybody here knows about it, or if they do, they don't ask. It's usually one-offs. Disappear out for the evening. My grandmother doesn't think much of us. She thinks that once she's gone, Peppa won't be much. My mum's away with it, if you know what I mean? Not quite on this planet. Gran feels she has to take charge, govern us all. Deal with everything.

'I'm sad that he's gone, Clive. He wouldn't have committed suicide. It wasn't about me. Something happened to him. I didn't want to say anything with Gran there. I don't want to come into the station and say anything. She'll hear about it. They'll all hear about it. I don't know what she'll do. She could soon put a clamp on me, stop me from going out. I know I'm twenty-two and I could leave, but I don't know how I could leave Mum. No money, you see. I've no funds, nothing. This is what I know how to do.' She pointed at the chicken poo on the ground.

'How long was it going on for?'

'He started going out to meet my mother regarding the egg farms. I think they were business discussions. That's what he told me. At that point, I saw it as a perfect opportunity. We were covered. Clive was really from the generation above although Jenna's his sister.

'It was the Tilburys, you see. Jenna, I grew up with. Myself and Jenna, Fern, then Alexis and Stephen. We all knew each other growing up. Clive and Roy were up above us. They didn't really bother with us at first until we got older and we could go down to the pub and then the pair of them started coming with us. Gran liked that in some ways, thought they were looking after us. Mum came down too, but Gran never thought she could look after us. She thought little of her at all. That's not healthy when you're growing up, to see your mother being disparaged all the time.'

'Why would your mother be making business discussions with Clive, then? Did she ever give you the impression that she had a thing for him?'

'My mother has a thing for everybody. No, I think it would be all business. She thinks she could run it. She always used to tell us that Gran only thought she was in charge. One day, it would all be hers. I'm not sure Gran liked that. Gran doesn't like the idea of giving up this place at all. Gran thinks she's the only one who can run anything.'

'What does Fern think?'

'Fern? Fern's a wide-eyed child. Six years between us and yet now she dresses like she thinks she is something. I don't know where she got that from. I think somebody was encouraging her. She wasn't like that a year or two ago.

'She was fourteen a couple of years ago. Maybe she wasn't that way inclined. Comes to us all at different ages,' said Susan.

'Not our Fern. She was a farming girl, always was. She could tell you more about these chickens than I ever could. Gran has great hopes for her. I had disappointed Gran as I would not go to an agricultural college. Didn't want to do any of that. I want out of this place. With Clive, I thought maybe that might happen. I didn't know. He was fun anyway, for the meantime. A little risky. I like risk. I like the idea of doing something different.

'If it blew up, I could rub it in Gran's face, couldn't I? Is there anything else you want to know? I've told you how it is. Keep me out of it. I don't want nothing to do with it. Clive's gone now, and it was an adventure. It was exciting. I'm sad he's gone, but I'm wise enough to keep my head.'

'Were you in love with him, then?' asked Susan.

'No, not really. Not with him. Just the idea that might have worked. He liked when I dressed up sexy. I have a figure, you know? I can use it. Get what I want. Get out of this place. What am I going to do here? Look at me. Walking through chicken shit. Wellington boots and jeans, big fluffy jumpers. Soon, I'll look like Gran. Worn hands, worn face.

'I want a life of ease. Not early mornings. Not wondering what the supermarket's going to demand of us next. I want a man to look after me. Comfort. Somewhere I get to do what I want. I've never had that. The farm comes first. Gran sees to that. The farm's always been the important thing. I sometimes wonder if she's lost it. That's what they grew up with. They don't see what we see. A chance to do something else. A chance to be something else.'

'I'll keep your secret safe for the moment,' said Susan, 'but I can't guarantee that it will stay that way in the long term. Somebody killed Clive, and somebody killed Roy. I've got to find them and bring them to justice. If your testimony is needed to do that, I'll seek it. I'll put you on a stand. I won't lie to you.'

'I won't say anything.'

'You may not get a choice but if we get evidence.'

'What evidence?'

'Wait and see. Just be aware that we can find things. Things turn up that say you were in certain places and then you're answering tough questions. If you say what you have just said to me, you won't have anything to fear from us, or from the judicial process.'

'Well, for now, I'm staying silent. Okay? Don't let anyone see you.'

Susan turned round and walked back out of the chicken barn. She glanced left and right, leaving it, staying tight to the buildings until she got back to the field. Crossing over, she walked round to her car. As she went to get inside it, she looked down at her feet. Her boots were practical because she was out working, but the bottom of them still had chicken poo on them. She wiped them through the grass repeatedly until it was gone.

I get Sarah, she thought. *I wouldn't want to walk in amongst dirt every day, smell that, hear the clucking and the squawking. Farm life was hard; that's what they all said. You rose early. Sometimes you were in bed late and you didn't make that much from it. What she said about the supermarkets was probably right as well.*

What was interesting, thought Susan, getting behind the wheel of the car, *was what she said about her mother. What exactly was going on at that meeting between Clive and Peppa, and where did he go afterwards?*

Susan drove away towards the station. Hope would be wanting to know how she got on.

Chapter 20

Ross pulled the car up at a small car park near the woods. Stepping out, he could feel that the rain was on the way. There was a slight dampness in the air and a few spits of rain. Perry got out from the other side, looked up, annoyed at the sky, and lifted the collar on his jacket.

'Do you not have any boots?' asked Ross. 'Some rain gear.'

'No.'

'You should try to grab something.'

'My stuff was sitting in my car. We're out in yours, and I haven't got transferred it over yet.'

Ross almost tutted. Opening the boot of his car, he lifted out a set of Wellington boots and a large waterproof jacket. He put them on and then marched off towards the woods, followed by Perry. As they walked, the rain got heavier, eventually turning into a downpour. Ross ignored the detective behind him and made his way to the bus stop before stopping and looking at the various paths one could take from there.

'So, she came here. Now, where would she go?'

'It's a pre-ordained meet,' said Perry. 'It's got to be somewhere they both know. I suspect they were doing this for a while, maybe. The first time she might have waited for him, not the second time. Get out of sight. They might even have somewhere regular.'

'What do you mean, regular? It's the woods.'

'Regular. If you're meeting for sex on a weekly basis, you're going to find somewhere.'

'Some sort of brick building, a shed, an old place for tool storage? I reckon they might even have made it comfortable.'

'No, I doubt you would do it inside a shed or anything. Too easy to get caught. You're trapped when you're inside a shed. Out in the open, somebody comes along, you can run.'

Ross was finding it disturbing that Perry seemed to know so much about this. He wondered what sort of woman would be interested enough in Perry to have gone to these lengths.

Perry tore off down a path which was mucky underfoot, and Ross had no choice but to follow him.

'Through here. Really obvious,' said Perry. 'But now you've come through the obvious, you're going to want to go somewhere more secluded. Don't follow the path. Don't follow the proper path.'

'Why not?' said Ross. 'You could go all the way down there and then cut off.'

'No. You don't want to be seen. Not at all, especially a young girl. Maybe he would, but if she's found a spot, it's going to be very secluded.'

'Why do you say that?'

'Because she's the one who's going to fear the most. Not him. He'll turn around and say it was her. If they get caught, though, he'll think he can handle it. Get them out of there before anything happens. She won't. She'll be afraid. They want to be together, but with a man that age, rumours will start. It's also the families' reactions. Things can end up very messy. It's something that can't be allowed. Remember, he's going on after this, going off to see her mum. She knows about that.'

'We don't know she does, do we?' said Ross.

'She's got to know. It's too neat, isn't it? I mean, really? He just pops along here and then he goes down there. It'd be a brilliant cover, wouldn't it? If he gets caught. If she's caught out and about, he can always blame it on having visited her mother. This is the only spot where he's in trouble. They've got to be very secretive once they get to the woods. This is where it all falls down.'

Ross watched as Perry suddenly disappeared in amongst trees. He pushed branches aside, creeping in and swearing occasionally when a stray branch hit him in the face.

'Are you just walking around at random?' asked Ross.

'No,' said Perry. He sounded annoyed.

'Are we really going to go through this hassle?'

'Yes,' said Perry. He paused and bent down, looking around him. 'Not here. You can be seen from that path over there. It's got to be somewhere close to here, though. Hang on.'

Crouched down to avoid branches, Perry wandered on and then was dropping to his knees. Ross thought the mud must be caking onto his trousers. For here, where the trees were thickest, the ground underneath was squelchy.

Perry pushed back a cluster of branches. 'Come here,' he said to Ross. Ross looked at him for a moment.

'Sir, come and have a look at this.'

Ross crept down as well but managed to not go to his knees. In saying that, there was a tremendous strain across him as he crouched. Getting close to Perry, he halted beside him.

'What?' asked Ross. Perry took a small flashlight pen out

of his pocket and shone it. Although it was still daytime, in here it was dark, not black as night, but Ross wondered what it would be like if it was nighttime. You'd be able to see very little. On the ground was a used condom.

'Can you go back a bit for me?' asked Perry. 'Go outside and see if you can see my pen torch.'

Ross climbed back out. Then he looked around, pushing back leaves.

'Just about if I move to the side of that.'

'This is it,' said Perry. 'This is it. Hang on a minute.'

He was still crouching when Ross came back towards him, but this time, like a crab, he'd gone sideways and now was reaching into a gap where a tree had rotted. His arm was halfway up the inside.

'What are you doing?' asked Ross.

Suddenly, Perry smiled. First, he pulled out several plastic bags, the sort that you'd have coal in. They were large and randomly up the tree. Then he pulled down an old blanket.

'If you're going to be doing it out here,' said Perry, 'you're going to need to be prepared. The first time they might do it, but the more often you come, the more prepared you're going to be. Wouldn't surprise me if they had a bit of tarpaulin or something to go over the top. It's very well sheltered. Very well, to a point. I wonder.'

'What do you mean, "you wonder?"' said Ross.

'Just a moment.' Perry went back like a crab and scuttled out the other side, and suddenly Ross couldn't see him.

'Just stay there. Stay right there,' said Perry.

'Why am I here?' Ross could hear the rain falling off the trees, dripping onto leaves. It was heavier now outside. Perry must be getting soaked. Ross looked around him. 'Are you still there? Where have you gone?'

'I'm still here. Don't worry,' said Perry. 'I'm not going anywhere.'

Ross looked around him. Do people seriously come to a place like this? They must be desperate. You could always just park a car up somewhere, but then a car could be identified. A car would be seen going places. The bus? You didn't see the bus, or you did, but it was always there. You'd have to be at the stop to see Clive get off.

'Are you still there?' shouted Perry.

'Where else am I going to go?' said Ross. 'Of course I'm still here. Why am I here?'

'Can you see me?'

Ross looked around. Despite being daylight outside, with small bits and pieces you could see through the leaves of the trees, it truly was dark. 'No,' said Ross, 'I can't.'

'Are you sure? Keep looking. A real proper look.'

Ross heard the voice. He turned his head in the direction it was coming from. 'No, not at all. I can't see a thing.'

'Well, that's interesting,' said Perry. 'I'll bring you around to look at this. Just be very careful.'

'Why?' asked Ross.

'Because I think somebody's been here.'

'That was the whole point,' said Ross.

'No, no. Not just Clive and Susan Brodie. Somebody else has been here. I think somebody's been watching them.'

It took about a minute before Perry was back beside Ross. Then he told him to follow him. It was hard going out from the leaves, but they got to a vantage point where Perry showed Ross that you could look down and you could see exactly where Ross had been.

'You come from back there. It's off the path. It's not that far away. I wonder,' said Perry.

'What?' asked Ross.

'You've been here several times,' said Perry, 'enough to set yourself up in a little makeshift bed. Maybe there's a bit of rain going on. Maybe there's some noise from the road, but you're comfortable. So instead of quietly going about your business, suddenly you're more excitable. I mean, they were having sex with each other. It wasn't a reading club or anything. There was going to be noise. You can imagine the first time they're silent, but if you haven't been caught week after week, you think like you're immune. You think people can't hear. If somebody who suspects you both is looking, and they see you, maybe they don't take to your little rendezvous. '

'It's conjecture though, isn't it?' said Ross. 'You're kind of making things up.'

'I'm running theories,' said Perry. 'There's nothing wrong with running theories. I know you need evidence to back things up, but you also need to see the people. You need to understand them.'

'How on earth do you understand them? Is this what you used to do? Were you running away with a younger woman like this?'

'Why do you say that?' asked Perry.

'You seem to know this too well. You seem to—'

'I get inside people's heads to try and understand why people do things. It's what I do. Come on, we need to go back towards the path here. Watch your feet. Don't walk that direct line.'

Perry turned, pushing branches aside, walking back, and then he halted. He was shining his pen torch down on the ground because the light was poor here as well, but Ross looked down and saw it. A footprint. An actual footprint.

'It's on the line, in the area. It's been protected by this tree, the leaves making a shelter.'

'We need to get you out of here now. We need to seal the whole place off.'

'I think you're right,' said Perry. 'Do you mind doing that?'

'Why?' asked Ross.

'Well, you know her better. I'm the new guy, and she won't send the best people out because she doesn't know who I am.'

'It's not a problem. You can ring her,' said Ross.

'Actually, I'm dying for a fag,' said Perry, coughing as if to point out his dilemma.

'Go smoke your fag, but stay well away from here,' said Ross. He turned back towards the car.

Ross called Jona, detailing the scene and the actions required. The condom could place Clive at the scene along with his lover. The footprint may offer a watcher. They would wait until forensics arrived and for some uniforms to come down and pick up the scene with him. After he finished the call, Ross didn't make his way back to Perry. Instead, he stood thinking.

The man clearly had talent. The man knew what he was talking about. How did he do that? Did he have something in his past? He certainly looked a seedy character.

Ross walked out towards the path where Perry was standing smoking. The man's jacket was absolutely sodden, the collar turned up. Perry's hair was tight to his head. The trousers were soaked through too, and his shoes, brown and suede, were as messed up as they could be. As Ross approached, Perry dragged hard on the cigarette and then blew smoke out in front of him.

'You seriously think someone was watching them then.'

'That's not just a random footprint.'

'We'll see. Possible evidence. If we can match it, it might put somebody else here. It's not conclusive, but it's a start. Like you said, we need to get some evidence together.'

Ross watched the man puffing on the cigarette and then putting it out under his foot.

'That was good work,' said Ross. 'I don't know how you do it. I don't know why you can understand the mindset of a man having sex with a much younger woman. You don't have experience, do you?'

'That's just a fantasy,' said Perry, turning to Ross. 'I'm on a detective salary. I haven't got the amount of money to justify that. They will not follow me for my good looks, will they?'

Perry looked a slob, but he was a slob-like genius, Ross decided.

'I'll tell Hope what you did here. Very good. Well done.'

Perry nodded at him. 'Does that mean I get an extra cigarette?'

'No,' said Ross. 'Come on. We need to help seal this place off, see what it brings us in the investigation. You only get the second cigarette when you crack the case.'

'That's a tempting offer.'

Chapter 21

Hope sat in her office, having just fielded a call from Ross and Perry. Jona was being dispatched to seal off the scene of possible copulation. Hope was waiting for Susan to return, spending her time in the office, running through what evidence they had.

Roy had been chatting with someone. It was bothering Hope. They needed to know who. She looked out from her office, across the team's office beyond, seeing only Davidson at the far end. She would be cataloguing more of the bus trips, and Hope wondered what it must have been like for Macleod.

At times, surely he would have sat like this, except he never had. Macleod liked to be out and on the go. Yes, he sent people out, but so often, he would go out himself. She wanted to go, too, but Hope had decided that Susan would be more effective, a better person, closer to the age group and able to get a rapport with Sarah Brodie.

Younger women could be like that. Somebody slightly older, somebody that looked like mum, didn't always wash with them. When did Hope start to not be the cool person around here? When was it that Hope became the older one? Macleod was always the fuddy-duddy, the one you didn't send in for the younger people. He knew that, same with Clarissa, although she was more eccentric, able to get away with it more. Macleod was dark, especially if you didn't know him, *mega-serious*.

As Hope pondered on this, Susan Cunningham entered the office, and went straight for Hope's door. She knocked quickly, and the door was opened before Hope could even say, 'Come in.'

'What's the news?' asked Hope, seeing Susan approach her.

'I didn't quite get a confession,' said Susan. 'Sarah spoke to me on the quiet. When I went there, Lorraine was very protective. Wanted to be with her at all times. Wanted me to interview Sarah in front of her. I talked about coming down to the station, but in the end, I felt it best if I stepped back.'

'What, you just left it?' asked Hope.

'No, I parked up elsewhere and watched for an opportune moment. I caught Sarah on her own, inside one of the chicken barns.'

'Nice,' said Hope. 'Was she more forthcoming?'

'She's not prepared to make a statement and said to me she won't say anything if she's being asked, down here or elsewhere. I think she's worried that she could be implicated. Not just that. Her mum obviously has some sort of feelings about Clive. I felt she believed her mum's not that stable.'

'What did she say?'

Basically, that Sarah and Clive indeed had sex, that they started it when her mum was meeting Clive. It was a perfect opportunity. They kept going. She thinks that only Clive and she knew about their rendezvous. She said that it was a shock to her when, well, he was killed.

'You don't think it's her, do you?' asked Hope.

'Not a chance. I think she was quite sensible with him. She

177

wanted the older man as she was looking for a way out. She's pretty sick of farming. Not surprising, really, when you look at it. They want the club; they want to be out and about. What's your image of farming girls?'

'Jumpers and jeans.'

'Exactly. Lambing. Farming. All quite tough work, or else big fat women in a kitchen. It's certainly not the clubbing girls, is it? Yet that's what Sarah and her sister want to be. That's the way they dress. The farming lifestyle just doesn't work the way they are. Maybe that will change over years, but at the moment, that's not them. Clive would have been an opportunity. Sarah thought he might take her out of it, give her a normal house. Clive could run the business. She wouldn't have to. She could get the home she'd want, free from responsibility.'

Hope's phone rang, and she picked it up. Susan sat, waiting for her boss to finish the conversation. When she did, Hope looked back at her.

'That's the techies. They've got into his computer and found the chats. They're trying to get us a list of them.

'MTB,' said Susan. 'I've been thinking about that. We need to crack it. We need to get our head together on this one.'

'It's got me. Somebody's obviously picked it for a reason. We need to get into their head. Why MTB? Why would I do that? What did it mean to anyone? It's clearly not the initials of anybody involved around Roy.'

'Why don't you bring down the brains of our outfit?' said Susan, and Hope raised an eyebrow. 'Whenever anyone talks about the boss, it's about how clever he is. Seoras has a way of seeing things. We could do with a bit of help on this one.'

Hope stood up and looked out the window. *Would this be her running to him? Would this be her not solving the case on her own?*

178

That wasn't what Macleod was about, though. Seoras had always said, 'First duty's to the case.' He didn't care what you looked like, didn't care if he was embarrassed. He just wanted to catch the killer. She needed to catch the killer.

Hope turned back to her desk, picked up the phone, and asked Macleod's secretary if he would come down.

It took Macleod two minutes to arrive at the office. Susan Cunningham, who had moved her chair off to one side, had placed one for Macleod, and he took it.

'I hope this isn't a delegation about Perry,' he said.

'What's wrong with Perry?' asked Susan.

'Good,' said Macleod. 'What's up?'

'Susan suggested I should ask you for a bit of help.'

'Right. I'm all ears.'

'Thing is, Seoras, we've got Roy Tilbury having late night chats. The chat says, "MTB", the person he's chatting with. We need to know who MTB could be. If Roy's having intimate chats, if this is Roy's love life, it could be the key.'

'First off, big assumption,' said Macleod. 'Is it his love life? Yes or no. Right, say it is, because otherwise, there's an entire part of his life we haven't even picked up on yet. Most people have some sort of, at least, friendship, a special person.'

'The only people Roy really sees are the young people when he goes out with them,' said Hope. 'Really, he's just there to cover off, isn't he? Gets him out of the house, there watching his sibling, Jenna.'

'Jenna's nineteen,' said Macleod. 'Why would I be going out to watch over my nineteen-year-old sister? She should be able to watch over herself by now.'

'There are arguments going on,' said Susan.

'Arguments going on amongst the women, the younger

women, at least,' said Macleod. 'What's the problem there?'

'One thing,' said Susan, 'was that Roy always kept this quiet. He's kept it away from his sister. He's kept it away from his mum.'

'Has he?' asked Macleod. 'Has he kept it away from his mum? You know his sister doesn't know it. I think we said that before in a meeting, and that's okay.'

'No, his sister didn't know what it was. She's the one I got it from.'

'His mum?' asked Macleod.

'Doesn't know about it as far as I know.'

'What would you keep away from everyone? MTB?' pondered Macleod.

Hope shook her head. 'What do you mean?'

'Let's make some assumptions here, ask what's wrong with this,' said Macleod. You talk with someone. We know it's fairly recent. It's not been going on for years. He's now talking to someone in a chat room. He keeps it very personal. It's never done on the company computers, only done on his. Only done in his room. It's kept on text chat. As far as we're aware, there's no video chat. He's not talking to anyone out loud. Why would you not talk to them out loud?'

'Because,' said Hope, 'somebody might overhear.'

'Yes. Somebody might overhear what?'

'The other person and identify them,' said Susan.

'That's certainly something,' said Macleod. 'Also—'

'They might identify something personal. Something relating to people they know about.'

'Exactly, Susan,' said Macleod. 'Somebody's using a code that is keeping it away from other people. They're not talking out loud because they could be identified. Have we got a secret affair going on? Possibly, if it indeed is an affair. Or it's a secret friend. What would you tell someone with the name, the tag in the chat, if you can't write their name down because mother or sister knows what their name is? You're going to want to know it's them. You're going to want it to be something very specific that only you know about them. Something maybe that's tying it all together.

Hope looked at Macleod. He had an almost smug grin to him because he'd cracked it. He'd actually cracked it. At least, he thought he had.

'Mum-to-be,' said Susan. 'MTB. Mum-to-be. Whoever it is, is pregnant. He doesn't want anybody else to know. They don't talk about it. They keep it in a chat room.'

'Mum-to-be,' said Macleod. We're looking for a mum-to-be. Also looking for the father of that child-to-be or somebody who would kill for what Roy had done to mum.'

'We know Sarah's promiscuous,' said Hope. 'She's been having this affair with Clive. Maybe she's playing about. Maybe that's why she doesn't want to make statements since Susan cornered her.'

'I'm not so sure. One thing that would help is if the techies check the chat and find the IP address,' said Susan.

'That should link back,' agreed Hope. 'You can get an IP address. Most chats are recorded these days. At least for a while. Legal reasons. In case something's said. In case of child abuse, grooming online. Things like that. They check, don't they? They have records. Certainly, they should have records that far back. Hasn't been a long time.'

Hope picked up her phone and called the techies, insisting that they try to get the IP address for the MTB, or mum-to-be, if indeed that's what it was.

'Already looking into it. It's not as easy as you make it out to be. We're in the computer and working on it now. We have to get careful, though. You can damage things quickly. Once you interfere, you've taken away the pristine example. Contaminated at that point.'

'I'm not here to tell you your job,' said Hope. 'But you could lead us to a murderer with this one. Best pace, please.'

Hope looked across her desk at Macleod. 'Thanks for that. I think we can handle it from here.'

'Good,' said Macleod. 'Just keep an open mind, though.'

'We know who the randy one is. We've got Peppa. Sarah being pregnant could ruin a lot of things for many people. Bit of a shock for somebody that old. He's nearly got twenty years on her—Roy. Somebody could kill him for it and try to make it look like the animal rights attacks that had happened previously. It all fits, Seoras. It all fits.'

'It's only conjecture at the moment,' said Macleod. 'Be aware of that. I've just made an educated guess. You need to get the evidence before you make the jump.'

'What's Clive got to do with it?' asked Susan suddenly. 'Clive's dead, but he's been having sex with Sarah as well. Does somebody think she's pregnant? Do they not know who the father is? Did they think it was Roy? Then they've bumped off Clive when they've realised he is actually the one.'

'When we get the chat IP address, when the techies tell us where it's come from, we'll have it,' said Hope. 'It's got to be one of two people in there, isn't it? You got Sarah, then you've got Fern. Fern is sixteen and shy, so that will not happen, is it? She doesn't really seem to go anywhere without her sister.'

Macleod turned and walked to the door. 'Tell me when you've wrapped it up then. I'll be listening. In your case, Hope, sensible to ask for advice, though. You used the surrounding resources.'

'You didn't seem to use the DCIs above you,' said Hope.

'I did,' said Macleod, 'but I didn't do it in front of a lot of other people. Some of them were good. Some of them were worth talking to. A couple of them, I went, and I shared a bacon sandwich with.' He closed the door as he went out, then he stopped and opened it again. 'Next time, I will expect coffee,' he said, 'especially if you're going to make me work.'

Hope saw Susan's grin. 'Don't you smile,' she said. 'You'll be the one making it for him.'

Chapter 22

Hope was up by her chair, almost bouncing around the office. Susan was still sitting in her chair with a slightly perplexed look on her face, but Hope could see the end of it all. She reached down to her desk and pressed a button, calling up Ross's mobile.

'Hang on a minute,' he blurted. She heard him sloshing around. It sounded like the rain was extremely heavy. 'Just getting in under some trees,' said Ross. 'What is it?'

'We've just cracked it. MTB from the chats. Had the boss down to help. Mum-to-be. Roy was talking to Mum-to-be. We reckon Sarah's pregnant. That's the secret. They killed Roy for it, but then she's been having sex as well with Clive, so they've killed him for it too. Someone must have known. Somebody must have seen. You see, Roy must have been having sex with her long before Clive.'

'Well, we got a footprint down here. All we have to do is start matching things up. Hang on. I'm just going to tell Perry.'

Hope heard Ross talking, relaying her theories over to Perry.

'Perry's not convinced,' said Ross. 'He's saying something about a condom.'

'Put him on then.'

'He's waving towards the car,' said Ross. 'We're going to get in the car and talk to you. I'll be able to put it on speakerphone then.'

Hope heard the man sloshing about and the rain hammering down. It seemed to get louder once they got inside the car, but Ross's speakerphone was put on and he exclaimed to her, 'All right, we've got Perry in here. Run it past him again.'

'Perry, MTB, Mum-to-be. Roy has got Sarah pregnant. She's also then gone into a relationship with Clive. Someone knows but could not identify who the father is. Thinks it's Roy, kills him, then realises that Clive's still sleeping with her.'

'No,' said Perry, 'no way. Sarah's using a condom here. We found it.'

'We found a condom,' said Ross. 'Could've been anybody's.'

'When Jona checks that through, we're going to find out that it's Clive's,' insisted Perry. 'Trust me, DNA will say Clive. Roy wasn't with Sarah. I don't think Sarah is pregnant. Why would she be having an affair with her mother's supposed boyfriend? Peppa wasn't in a relationship with Clive. And if she's admitted to you she's been with Clive, why wouldn't Sarah admit to being with Roy? Why not? If she's trying to put herself in the clear but doesn't want to go on record, she'd tell you everything to get you off her back so you wouldn't keep coming around. No, I don't agree with this. She's not pregnant.'

'She doesn't look pregnant either,' said Ross.

'You don't have to look pregnant to be pregnant,' said Hope. 'Some people go nearly full term before they even realise. Some people have actually given birth without realising.'

'I don't like it,' said Perry. 'I don't think we're right on this one. Sarah is secretive, but Sarah is careful. Roy? No.'

'Well, we should be able to get a link through from the chat room, get the IP address. I mean, we should be able to find at least what house it's coming from, accounts as well. We could just go in and seize everything. Seize all the laptops,' said Hope.

'We need to be careful,' said Ross. 'We make a move like that, and everybody knows the angle we're going at. I think we need harder evidence.'

'But it's here,' said Hope. 'We've got this in front of us. We've got evidence; we've got the pieces. It's just they're all scrambled. These are scrambled eggs we've got. We need to put them back to where they were before they were all whipped together.'

'We'll get on here,' said Ross, 'see what Jona can dig up. When we get the boot print, we'll be able to look and see who's got a similar boot print. That's hard evidence. We know someone was here; someone saw them.'

'I don't think the person who was looking at them has a clue we'll be onto them, and don't mention it to Sarah,' said Perry. 'Keep her in the dark about this. We keep the footprint in the dark. Look for it on the quiet. If we put it out there, we'll flag it up like a red rag to a bull. They'll just ditch the shoe. Whoever's doing this thinks they're covered, thinks people haven't been able to see them.'

'Question,' said Susan, 'what makes us think it's the same killer?'

'Well, it fits the idea, Susan,' said Hope.

'It's still conjecture. We still don't know if she's pregnant. Are we going to ask her? We can't force her to do a test. She will not admit to anything, evidence back out the window. We could end up getting stagnated over somebody who isn't at the heart of this case. I don't think we should move too quick,' said Susan.

'We have got two people dead.'

'Indeed,' said Susan to Hope, 'but if you're all right, who else is going to be killed? If they've seen Clive with her and they think they got Roy wrong and then killed Clive, they think it's done, don't they? No reason to kill anybody else.'

'Susan's talking a lot of sense,' said Perry. 'I really don't like this line of attack, boss.'

'What do you think, Ross?' asked Hope.

'We might be right on the Mum-to-be, what the words mean, but I don't know. I've got no hard evidence. This is conjecture,' said Ross. 'You know me. We need to get something concrete. Computer's the way to go, build our evidence up that way.'

'We can't wait either,' said Perry. 'What if this isn't someone going after the fathers? What if it ends up being Susan or the Mum-to-be as well?'

'I would say don't move yet,' said Ross. 'Let's get this shoe print—go along those lines.'

'I have to disagree,' said Perry. 'Go to the people. We'll work it out from them. The shoe print will be substantial evidence if it actually belongs to the person who was watching. I could be wrong with that. I knew I was right with where they were meeting, knew they were having sex. The shoe print is there. I didn't foresee somebody coming to watch them. I don't know who to suspect of watching, boss,' said Perry. 'Let's be careful charging in. I think you need to sit back and look at the people. Think about the way people have been with you when you've been speaking to them.'

'Understood,' said Hope. She turned around and gave a grimace towards Susan. 'We're going to have a think about it. I'll contact you. Get Jona on that footprint, though. I want to go with that. I want it with us when we next speak to our farmers.

Hope went out from behind her desk, and told Susan to get something to eat because that's what Hope was going to do. Susan asked if Hope would join her and Hope shook her head.

'No, I need to think,' she said. She made her way downstairs to the canteen, though, picked up dinner, and brought it back up on a tray to her office. She sat down, looking at the fish in front of her, slowly cutting off the first bit, and then taking a bite. It was good. It was hot. She finished her food, turned, and stared out the window.

What is it? she thought *What is it?* Hope picked up the phone and called John. He was surprised when she called.

'I want to run something past you,' she said.

'Okay.'

'Say you were having an affair on me and it's another woman and you've got her pregnant. Would you keep her at a distance?'

'Wow,' he said. 'I don't know. I'm hoping it will not be an issue.'

'But would you?'

'It depends, doesn't it? Does she want it to be known she's pregnant? I'd want to look after the child. I'd want to provide for it, but that's really her call, isn't it?'

'What if she was younger, much younger than you? Would you want to keep it secret?' asked Hope.

'I guess it depends on those around, doesn't it? Depends how families will react, what the stakes would be.'

'And what would the stakes be?' said Hope. 'I mean, for you personally.'

'Blimey, what is this?' said John. 'I mean, there's plenty of stakes, isn't it? There'd be you for a start, so if you've got a significant other, you're going to have to think what they will think. You could be in danger of losing them, if you still care about them, of course, given that you've gone off and had a baby with someone else. You've got to think about your business, your life. What about friends at the squash club?'

'The squash club?'

'The yacht club, the squash club, I don't know. I don't know who this person is or what age they are. I don't know what things they're into, what job they're in. Jobs can be funny things. Some people identify by their jobs, don't they?'

'Yes, they do,' said Hope. 'Some people identify by their jobs. How much does that job mean to you?'

'That's unfair,' said John, 'asking me that, but I wouldn't get into trouble because why would I want to mess around? I've got you.'

'Imagine you didn't have me. You're lonely. Imagine you were getting to the age of forty and you haven't got someone. Would you want someone, and would it be okay to bring them into the light?'

'Well, it depends, doesn't it? Depends on the sort of person you are. This is not like you. You're normally much more on top of stuff. You don't ask me about cases.'

'I've asked many people recently, had Macleod in. I've got a mess, John, a big mess to do with these egg farms. Scrambled eggs is what I've got. Eggs that have been whipped up and now you look at them, they look all yellow on top of their toast and you can't see the differences. What did they look like before? What was mixed with what first? I need to get back to the basic ingredients. I need to understand the eggs that were put in.'

'But eggs are all just the same, aren't they?'

'Not these ones,' said Hope. 'I don't know when I'll be back,' she said suddenly. 'I need to have a think about this.'

'You need to get yourself in a place where you can think. Go for a walk, do something. Do what you do.'

Hope placed her phone back down, and it rang again almost instantly. Answering it, she realised it was the techie she'd spoken to earlier.

'I'm calling you back because you said that we needed to trace through. There's a VPN, a virtual private network on it. It's hard to trace back to the original source. We can get to the private network, the VPN. I can't find beyond it. It's bouncing about here, there, and everywhere. Maybe we will get there, eventually. Not at the moment. I'm sorry, but this is tough. I can print the chats out for you. You can see if any of it makes sense.'

'From what you've seen so far,' said Hope, 'would it say that you're talking to a pregnant woman on one end and a man needing to either cover that up on the other?'

'I'm no detective,' said the man, 'but what I will say is that's not obvious. Maybe you'll see it from a conversation. The conversation's rather banal in some ways.'

'Well, keep on it,' said Hope. She put the phone down, stood up, and looked outside the window. *This is what Macleod did*, she thought. *Stand here and look out. He said the view was tremendous.*

Hope stood for another minute and a half, and then she shook her head. *This is what Macleod did. I need to do what I do. What do I do?*

She thought about what Perry had said, but wasn't for rocking the boat. Suddenly it dawned on Hope that while

Perry may have been good at looking at people, judging them, sitting back and thinking about motives, that wasn't Hope. Hope put the boots on the ground. Hope went and chivvied people. Susan wasn't back from dinner. Well, she would not wait. Hope walked over to her coat rack and threw on her leather jacket.

Macleod kept me because of me, because of what I was. Stop trying to become him, thought Hope. *I'm the DI who gets on out there, who goes and shakes things up. I'm the DI who's going to follow the process. Who possibly knew about Roy's chat? Jenna, but we've spoken to her, and she's admitted it. Mum? Maybe Esme caught her son in the act. Maybe she'd seen things. She'd been the only one in and out of his room. Not necessarily, there was his father. I'll go have a chat with Esme. Find out what she knows. I need to unscramble these eggs and that will not happen unless I've given them a shake!*

She opened her office door, stepped through, and closed it behind her. She looked down at the line of empty desks in the office with Davidson at the far end.

'Found anybody else on the CCTV?' she asked Davidson.

'No, no one of interest.'

Hope nodded. She made her way down the stairs towards her car. It was time to take the investigation in hand. Time for her to lead from the front. Time to find out who did this.

Chapter 23

Hope drove with a new purpose right towards the Tilbury farm, determined to see Esme. She didn't have a child of her own, though clearly Hope wanted one, but she'd heard some say that mothers know their children well. Esme would know what was going on, surely. Would Roy have been able to hide his secrets from her? Maybe, for he was a grown man. Yet, Hope got the feeling Esme was not a naïve woman to be pushed aside.

When she arrived at the Tilbury farm, she could still see the wreckage of the fires. She followed the road on round to the farmhouse, which looked quiet. The entire farm looked quiet. Almost eerie.

On the other farms she had visited, there was a business to them. Farmhands here and there, the clucking of chickens. The Tilbury farm was just a charred mess.

Hope got out of the car with the rain falling down all around her, but she pulled her leather jacket around her tight and ran through the rain up to the front door. She banged on it to hear a 'Coming' from inside. It wasn't a positive shout, more a resentful one from someone who didn't want to be disturbed. The door opened and Donald Tilbury stood on the other side.

'Mr Tilbury,' said Hope, 'I was looking for your wife.'

'Esme's gone off into town,' he said. His shoulders were slumped and he wore the air of a man who was defeated.

'Have you been able to make a start in dealing with the farm?'

'What do you think? It's just a mess. It's just a complete sodding mess.'

Hope heard a car pulling up behind her. She had called Susan, advising her where she was going. Hope turned to Donald.

'Stay there,' she said, and walked back to Susan Cunningham. Cunningham rolled down the window.

'Go find Jenna,' said Hope. 'Donald says that Esme has gone into town. He didn't say for what. Just check that with Jenna if you can.'

Hope turned and walked over to Donald. 'Come with me a minute,' she said. 'I've got something I need to talk to you about.'

Hope took the man round to the side of the house, where they had a view of the destroyed barns. The blackened shells were clear, some structures barely holding on. There was no life about them, no chickens.

'Does the insurance pay for this?' asked Hope.

She cast a glance over her shoulder as she asked Donald the question and saw Susan Cunningham disappearing up to the house.

'Insurance? No, not for something like this. I don't think it will cover it. I don't think we'll get back up on our feet. The effort to do it, and Roy's gone. Why would I want to do this again? I built it up. Roy was going to take it over.'

'Jenna will not take it on?'

'Roy was the one. Jenna's an afterthought. Jenna will be a good wife for someone. Roy was the boy. Roy was the man to

193

do it.'

Hope continued to ask some rather vague questions about insurance and about land rights, which Donald seemed happy to engage her with. By rights, he should have been fed up. He shouldn't have answered them at all. Hope felt her heckles going up and a glance over her shoulder told her that Susan Cunningham had returned to the car.

'Well, thank you for your time, Mr Tilbury. I'll see if I can find your wife in town. Much appreciated.' Hope strode towards Susan Cunningham's car where Susan rolled down the window.

'Jenna says she doesn't know where her mum is, but she had no plans to go into town, not that she'd heard of.'

'Okay,' said Hope. 'We go, but we stay very close by. I don't like it when I don't know where people are.'

Following Susan Cunningham's car, Hope exited the Tilbury farm and then parked up on the main road in a lay-by along with Susan.

'Ross,' said Hope after sending a call through to him.

'We're still here. This rain is shocking,' said Ross, 'a real pain.'

'How's Jona getting on?' Hope asked.

'We should have a scan of the footprint from here soon, going out to everyone. What's the matter?'

'I've gone looking for Esme and Donald says she's in town, but I'm not happy. Something doesn't feel right up there, especially when I was talking to Donald. I want you to go to the Daniels, and Perry to go to the Brodies.'

'We're both here in the same car.'

'Fine, I'll get Macleod to do it.'

'You want to borrow the boss?' queried Ross. 'You've got Susan with you. She could pop up.'

'Something's not right,' said Hope, 'but we're going to take action. We're going to find everyone. Two dead already. Something's on the go by the way Donald spoke to me. Jenna not knowing her mother's going into town, as well. Something just isn't right.'

'We'll get on the move then,' said Ross. Hope closed that call and opened up another one to Macleod.

'Everyone's out and about, Seoras. I need you.'

'What's up?' he asked.

'I'm over at the Tilburys. I spoke to Donald because I've been looking for Esme. Esme will know about Roy. She'll know what's going on with the computer chat rooms. She'll have an idea, but apparently, she's gone to town. Susan asked Jenna and Jenna says her mum had no plans.

'The way Donald spoke to me, answering annoying and bland questions that, by all rights, he should have told me to clear off with. After all, he's a man in mourning, but he answered them so happily, so straightforward, as if these were reasonable. Ross and Perry are out together. I've sent them to the Daniels. I need you to cover off Brodies. Just make sure everybody's there.'

'Where's Cunningham?' asked Macleod. 'I've got a meeting coming up. I'd rather not go out unless—'

'Cunningham's with me, Seoras. Trust me on this one. I need you. I'm not happy and I think something's happening. Just can't see what. I can't get to the bottom of this, so I'm doing what I do. Stepping out and taking action. I'm going to find people. If I know everybody is where they should be, I'll be happy. But if not, we'll sort this out.'

'Good,' said Macleod, 'I didn't want to be in that meeting, anyway. I'm on my way.'

Hope closed down the call and looked over at Cunningham. 'Susan, let's get back in the car. Get up as close to that farm as we can just in case; we can spot someone who shouldn't be there.'

Cunningham smiled back, 'Yes, boss,' she said.

Scene break, scene break, scene break.

Ross pulled his car up in front of the Daniels's farm. It had a solemn air to it, albeit that work was still going on out amongst the chickens. Along with Perry, Ross approached the front door of the house and was told by young Stephen that his grandfather was out at one of the chicken barns. Perry and Ross walked over, arriving at the first one, and were then told by a farmhand that Bernard was in the second. They knocked on the door and Bernard opened it in a blue boiler suit.

'Have you any news about what happened with Clive?' he asked.

'Not yet. We're still investigating.'

'I thought I'd just get back to doing something. I can't stay in the house. Stephen's so sombre, so quiet. He's not really speaking since it happened, and as for Alexis, she just keeps holding me. Keeps asking if I'm okay. I should be there for her, not the other way round.'

'I've seen these things too many times, sir,' said Ross. 'Everybody takes it differently. Everyone has their own way. There's no right or wrong.'

'He's right,' said Perry. 'If she wants to look after you, let her. It's her way of coping like you are here, out amongst your chickens, looking after them. Bring her out here.'

'That would be a good idea. We could work away together,

just be around each other.'

'I'm afraid I have to ask you some questions,' said Ross. 'It's regarding Clive. We now know Clive was meeting with Peppa Brodie. Were you aware of that?'

'Yes,' said Bernard. 'I was, but in truth, I didn't want to say anything about it because he had told me it in confidence. Why do you ask about her?'

'The night he died, he was seeing her. Are you not aware?'

'I didn't know when they met. He'd said to me on the quiet that she was looking to broker a business deal. He didn't want to upset anything. Clive had done well. He wanted to make the farm bigger. He wanted to see if we could take on other farms.

'To openly be negotiating or talking about one would have been poor business. It would have put the others off if we then approached them, or it might have sent them into a flutter, pre-warned them. They might have made unrealistic requests. Clive was a shrewd businessman, but it was my business, albeit that he was running it of late. So yes, he told me.'

'He met her in a pub that night before he died, and apparently, they had been having regular meetings,' said Ross.

'It had been going on for a month or two,' said Bernard, 'but Clive said it was business and she wasn't really offering much new. He had gone along and tried to negotiate, but he was starting to feel she wasn't really there with Lorraine's blessing. More like she was trying to negotiate about something she didn't really control.

'Clive was clever. He was always on about business. He knew his numbers inside out. If you'd gone to him and you didn't know what you were talking about, he would know. He'd said to me recently that he'd asked her several times for more numbers about the business, about plans, about intentions. At one point, he'd asked her was Lorraine behind all this, and Peppa said that no, she was going to be taking over the business, and that's why he was talking to her.'

'Did he mention,' asked Ross, 'how she dressed when she went to these meetings?'

'No, I don't think so,' said Bernard. 'He went fairly casually. He was keen not to be seen disappearing out wearing a suit because that would have been a business meeting. Clive wasn't a fashionable dresser. Clive was just farm orientated. That's the way he was, so when he went to talk business, he went in a suit, shirt, and tie. Nothing flash. But this was meant to be business on the quiet.'

'And he didn't ever give an indication how she dressed?'

Bernard stared off into the ceiling of the barn, clearly casting his mind back.

'Yes,' he said. 'Yes, he did. I remember it now, throwaway line. He said at the first meeting that she sat forward, felt she was trying to use her womanly charms against him. Said it was ridiculous because he wasn't interested in her, anyway.'

'Not at all?'

'No. In fact, he said, "She's not the one I'm interested in."' Bernard paused. 'I always thought he had another flame on the go, possibly, but I guess not. Maybe it was just someone he fancied. Silent on that side of things. A bit like myself. I don't wear my feelings on my sleeve.'

'Thank you,' said Ross, and began to walk away.

'Sad, isn't it?' said Perry. 'But one thing's clear, Peppa is up to something. She talked about an affair. She talked about them getting together.'

Ross pulled his phone out as he felt it vibrating in his pocket and noticed that Perry had done the same. They both looked down and got the same message. Jona had sent a scan of the type of tread on the sole of the shoe that had made the mark in the soil. Had someone been watching? Clive and Sarah would have been unaware.

Ross placed a call through to Hope. 'I'll tell the boss what's going on. We'll need to get over to the Brodies. Something's wrong. Something's not right.'

Ross closed the call down shortly after and Perry looked at him.

'Hope says we're to stay put. Keep eyes on everyone here. Apparently, Macleod has gone over to the Brodies.'

'She's brought in the big guns, then,' said Perry.

'Do you think it's like that? You think she can't cope?'

'No,' said Perry. 'Where is our esteemed inspector at the moment?'

'She's still at the Tilburys.'

Perry stood for a moment. Then he pulled out a cigarette, lit it, and began to smoke.

'No wise comment?' said Ross. 'You just think that she's brought Macleod in to solve it all?'

'You think so little of me,' said Perry. 'Even after I find the love den in the woods. Inspector McGrath is exactly where she needs to be, and I think she knows it. Deep down, I think she knows it.'

Chapter 24

Seoras Macleod pulled up in his car at the Brodie Farm. This had been an investigation he'd seen from a distance, never being up close with any of the suspects, but he knew that this was coming. He had been tempted to leap in when Hope said they needed another body, but he'd gone and got her Perry.

She needed to run this herself, needed to solve it. Not be hanging on to him or having him around her. She was an inspector now, the real one, and this was her case. That being said, he was buzzing inside.

Seoras was meant to have a budget meeting that afternoon. Macleod was worried it was going to go on until seven or eight o'clock at night. Instead, he was out here. He took great delight in the phone call, refusing to let his secretary cancel the meeting, but instead to call through himself.

He was proud of Hope, for she had told him she needed him, but exactly where and why. She wasn't looking for her big brother to come down and help, rather she just knew she needed someone of a certain calibre. This wasn't how he would've solved it, but it was her way, and he was in on it.

Macleod stepped out of the car and saw a rather fierce

woman looking at him. She was maybe heading towards her sixties, close to his age, but she had a grimace that could make a grown man shrink.

'Who might you be?'

'I'm Detective Chief Inspector Seoras Macleod.'

'Really?'

'I've been asked to come by Inspector McGrath. I take it you would be Lorraine Brodie.'

'They gave you the smarts when they put you to the top,' said Lorraine. 'We're quite busy here today. I hope you don't mind going back to the office.'

'I mind greatly, especially if I don't get what I'm here for.'

'What is that?'

Macleod stopped talking suddenly. There was a nearby open window in the house and he thought he heard someone throwing up. 'Someone not well?' he asked.

'Fern's not well, that's my daughter's younger girl.'

'The younger of two, the other being Sarah?' said Macleod. 'Perhaps it's your daughter. Don't worry. I've been fully involved in the investigation.' *Or at least fully made aware of it.* 'What's the matter with her?'

'She's just not feeling well. Grandma's looking after her,' said Lorraine.

'How long has she been ill for?' said Macleod.

'Very recent. You could still get tummy bugs at sixteen,' said Lorraine.

'You don't mind if I go inside then, just to make sure she is there.'

'I do mind,' said Lorraine. 'I've got business to get on with.'

'Look, I am Detective Chief Inspector Macleod. I am here because it is important. I hope to make sure all of your family are safe. If you let me come in and see Fern and then see Peppa and Sarah, we'll be all right. I'll leave you alone. But if you refuse, I'll go about my business in a more autocratic way.'

Macleod glared at the woman and for a moment he felt like he was going toe to toe with a boxing legend, but he must've cut a splendid figure because she relinquished.

'This way then, Detective Inspector.'

'Detective Chief Inspector,' said Macleod. Lorraine nodded. *Yes, she knew!* Macleod followed her through the front door, then towards the kitchen.

'You'll forgive me if I don't drag you into the bathroom to see my granddaughter. Give her a bit of privacy.'

'Of course,' said Macleod. 'You can see if she's all right, and bring her out. As I said, I'm here to make sure everyone's safe.'

'Why wouldn't they be safe? My farm; I know what I'm doing.'

'Yes,' said Macleod. 'The only farm that has lost no one so far.'

'What's that meant to mean?'

'There isn't any man here, is there?' asked Macleod.

Macleod stood in the kitchen, watching as Lorraine walked off towards where he suspected the bathroom was. He heard the door open, and then saw the returning Lorraine's confused face. Shortly after, a woman of around forty walked in.

'You're not Fern,' said Macleod. 'I take it this is Peppa.'

'This is my daughter,' said Lorraine. She ran her hand through her white hair, looking slightly distressed.

'Where's Fern?'

'I don't know,' said Peppa.

Lorraine looked down at the floor. 'I've told you before about walking through here with your muddy footprints.

Leave your boots out when you come back from the chickens.'

'I didn't have time. I needed the toilet, okay? Didn't feel great.'

Macleod looked down at a footprint left on the kitchen floor. He took out his phone and glanced at the shoe cast print sent through by Jona. Certainly, the boot prints seem to match. However, he put his phone back into his pocket.

'Do you know where Fern is?'

'Where is she?' said Lorraine. 'She wasn't well. I said before she needed looked after.'

'I haven't seen her. I thought she was in the house the whole time,' said Lorraine.

'Where's Sarah?' asked Macleod. 'Get Sarah here now, please.' Peppa went to turn away, but Macleod said, 'No, you stay here. Lorraine, go get your granddaughter.'

As Lorraine left, Macleod turned to Peppa. 'Can you take your boots off, please? I believe your mother doesn't want muddy footprints, so just leave them over there.'

Macleod pointed to the corner. Peppa looked at him rather bemusedly. Macleod nodded softly, showing she should comply. As Peppa was putting the boots into the corner of the kitchen, Lorraine came back in with Sarah.

'She said she hasn't seen her.'

'Sarah, I'm Detective Chief Inspector Macleod. Where is Fern?'

'I haven't seen her.'

'When was the last time she was seen?'

'I saw her last night. She hasn't been up this morning,' said Sarah.

'Lorraine, you said you were looking after her. She wasn't well,' cried Peppa.

'I haven't seen her since last night, either,' said Lorraine. 'I told her to keep her head down. Told her to.'

'You haven't seen her since when, Peppa?' asked Macleod.

'Last night, too,' said Peppa. 'She's not sick, is she?' said Macleod, 'at least not from a virus or anything. She's being sick for another reason.'

He saw Lorraine's wide eyes staring back at him and knew he was right.

'Show me her room,' said Macleod.

Lorraine strode out of the kitchen and up the stairs. Macleod was taken along the ground floor past the bathroom next to Fern's room. Lorraine knocked on the door and then she opened it. The bed had been slept in, or at least disturbed. Macleod looked around it, then went over to the ground-floor window.

It led out to the side of the house. The inside had its catch hanging loose. Macleod tore out of the house and went to the side to see the window. Once there, he could see the tell-tale marks of a window having been forced open. He marched back inside.

'How old's that window?'

'Years old. It's not that solid, but it does.'

'Not this time it hasn't,' he said. 'All three of you, sit down in this kitchen.'

Macleod walked over and stood beside the pair of boots on the kitchen floor. He picked up his mobile and called Hope.

'Hope, we're missing one of the Brodies. It's Fern. I believe she's pregnant, and believe she's at the cause of all this, or at least half of it. I've got a pair of boots here to solve the other half. Search the Tilbury farm. You need to find Fern and you need to find her quick.'

Scene break. Scene break. Scene break.

Hope closed down the call and turned to Cunningham. 'Fern's pregnant. She's been taken and the boss thinks she's here. We need to search the farm. Go.'

Cunningham put her foot down, racing the car in from outside and up the driveway. As she pulled up in front of the house, Hope was still on the phone calling the station for backup, to send as many as possible out. Cunningham was first up to the door of the house. It was locked. She rang the doorbell, banging on the door frame as well. It was opened ten seconds later, and Jenna looked back at her.

'Where's your parents?' asked Susan.

'They told me they had to do something. Some sort of audit up round the burnt down barns. Told me to stay in. Said they'd be back in an hour or an hour and a half. Dad seemed really sombre. He was—'

'He was what?' asked Susan.

'It's the loss of his chickens. He didn't want to go back up there. He said there'd been enough killing. There'd been enough going on. I can't imagine what it's like for him. He lost them all. He lost—'

'Where did they go?'

'The barns.'

'Which ones?'

'I didn't see them leave. They told me to stay in my room. Then you banged the door like anything 'What's wrong?' asked Jenna, nervously. 'What's happening?'

Hope had just come off the phone and saw Cunningham pointing up to the barns. 'Up there,' she said. 'I think they've gone up there.'

Hope ran, with Cunningham coming up behind her. As much as she was younger, Cunningham didn't have the pace that Hope had. This was Hope's case. This was her neck on the line. Her head had the image of a sixteen-year-old girl, but more than that, a pregnant sixteen-year-old girl. The rain was still pelting down and Hope splashed through the muddy field.

She saw the barns, wondering where they would hide. Most of them were destroyed, flattened, completely levelled. They couldn't be in there. That wouldn't work.

She saw one sitting slightly further back. The side of it had survived the blaze. From where she looked, it would still provide some sort of shelter as the rain drove in against the walls.

Where else would they go? Up into the woods? This barn was a reasonable guess, thought Hope.

She tore off towards it. As she got closer, Hope could smell something burning. There had been a general smell of a spent fire in the air during the entire investigation, but no, this smelt fresher, and Hope raced to the door.

As she looked inside, she stared up in horror. Fern was hanging from one of the beams that remained up towards the roof of the barn. Her wrists were tied together, and she was hanging from them. The girl's top was hauled up and her belly had been marked, though Hope wasn't sure what with. Her feet were a good two feet off the ground and she was swaying as fire burnt around her.

It was sweeping through a bed of wood underneath, one that had been clawed, broken up, and taken from the burnt shell around them. Hope went to race through the door towards her, but someone hit her hard in the back. She crumpled to the ground, turned and looked up to see Donald with a two-by-four about to bring it down on her head. Hope put both arms up, desperate to prevent him, but she saw the swing about to happen.

As Donald swung down, he was hit in the side, a shoulder clattering into him, taking him down to the ground. Cunningham was rolling over with him, and Hope saw her get up to her knees. She went to restrain the man when from somewhere behind the wall, a woman ran out screaming.

'My son is dead because of her. She did it. Temptress. Evil.'

Cunningham was hit in the back by another piece of wood. Hope thought about helping her, but the flames were now licking high up, and Fern was screaming. Had she been knocked out earlier? Hope didn't know, but what she knew was the girl's clothes were catching fire.

Hope ran over, stepping over the burning wood beneath her feet. The flames licked up, causing her to turn her head away from them. She'd have to be quick. This would all in an all-encompassing blaze in no time.

Hope couldn't pull her down because the girl's hands were tied tight above her. Instead, Hope jumped up, throwing her arms around Fern, clambering up her, like she was part of a rope. As she reached Fern's hands, Hope hung on with one hand, reached inside her jacket, and grabbed a pocket knife.

Fern screamed as the flames grew higher and Hope tried to ignore the heat driving towards them. She worked at the rope, cutting as hard as she could. It sliced through, the blade catching Fern's wrist as well, causing her to scream. The two women tumbled down into the burning wood.

Hope landed on her back, rolled over as quick as she could, and grabbed Fern's clothing. At six feet tall, Hope had a strength most women didn't, and she picked the girl up, one hand on her top, the other on the leggings she wore. Hope ran through the flames, the blazing wood underneath her feet, throwing a flame covered Fern and herself to the remnants of burnt chicken poo beyond.

Hope rolled over, putting out the small flames which had caught her clothes. Then she turned on her knees and patted down Fern, whose leggings were on fire. Satisfied they'd gone out, Hope tried to stand and look over towards Susan Cunningham.

Last she'd seen, Cunningham had been hit in the back with a piece of wood, and Esme was still coming for her. But Cunningham was now standing tall. Donald was lying on the ground, face down, Cunningham's boot on the small of his back. Across from her, Esme was sporting a bloody mouth. Cunningham smiled and Hope could see the blood running down her cheek.

'I got it,' she said. 'I got it.'

'You okay?' asked Hope.

'Just call the damn ambulance. That's a pregnant woman you just dropped in the fire.'

Hope made a grab for her phone and could hear the scream of sirens as backup arrived at the farm.

Chapter 25

It was two in the morning when the team was finally gathered all together back at the station. Everything wasn't quite wrapped up, but it was for the night. Lorraine Brodie was in a cell having been arrested for the murder of Roy Tilbury. Peppa Brodie had been arrested for the murder of Clive Daniels. Donald and Esme Tilbury had been arrested for the attempted murder of Fern Brodie. Hope and Cunningham had come back, along with Ross and Perry, and were now sitting in Hope's office. Macleod had been involved as well, writing up a statement of what he'd found. Jona and her team had been out, and everyone was feeling exhausted, having dealt with all the preliminary paperwork. The rest would come in the days to follow.

Hope had brought Davidson in as well, the one member of the team who hadn't been involved with the exciting conclusion. As Hope sat on the edge of her desk, Davidson took in every word about the scrambled eggs and how they'd all started out.

'It was quite simple, really,' said Hope, almost causing Ross to bust out laughing. Roy Tilbury was lonely as any man of his age would have been. The Brodie youngsters, Sarah, and Fern, dressed to impress and were obviously out for some fun. Clive was also taken in by them. The other young woman, Alexis, made the final temptress of the three of them, and Roy and Clive were taken in.

'Jenna was Roy's sister, and her being there made everything look normal. Clive and Roy were just looking after them. Stephen was there too, but when they were all meeting down in the pub, relationships were developing. Roy, at some point, had developed a relationship with Fern that ended up in her getting pregnant. MTB, mother-to-be, was Fern.

Lorraine Brodie was a woman who understood her house and those around her. She could see that Fern was pregnant, knew it, and found out who had got her pregnant. Lorraine killed Roy. She was well acquainted with how the farms worked, so it wasn't difficult to have trapped him and then taken him inside the barns. She knew from her daughters being in the group, roughly where he would be, what time they would leave. It was a recognised pattern.

'And nobody would look for Lorraine. Lorraine would be in bed. She killed Roy for getting Fern pregnant. She said she knocked him out, then took him round to the farm, in with the chickens, and set everything up for the incendiaries. It had been a while in the planning, several weeks, but she's a wily character.'

'Very,' said Macleod. 'You did well to catch her.'

'She also hid Fern's pregnancy from everyone else. Fern was quiet after Roy died—scared, because of the hold Lorraine had on her.'

'What happened with Clive, then?' asked Davidson.

'Well,' said Hope, 'the thing with Clive was, he also got taken in by one of the Brodie youngsters, except this one was Sarah.

However, Peppa, Sarah's mother, thought that Clive would fall in love with her, and they'd bring the farms together. Peppa was fed up with being controlled, dominated, ordered about by Lorraine. She wanted to be the mistress of the man.

'However, Clive wasn't interested in her, so she came up with a business meeting. It would be a secret one because there was talk about amalgamating the farms. It would have to be done on the quiet, so she met Clive regularly, once a week for a while. Clive saw this as business, and over time, actually wondered if Peppa had any idea what she was doing.

'Peppa also must have got wind that Clive wasn't interested and maybe there was someone else. She was fixated on him. At some point, she followed him because Clive had started having sex with Sarah, but he was clever about it. He was disappearing to go on the bus to then meet Peppa at their secret meeting. He had told his father, Bernard, that he was doing this. If he got caught out, he could say it was to do with Peppa and Bernard would back him up, but in the hours beforehand, he was going out to meet Sarah.

'They met in the woods, and in fairness to Perry, he was spot on. Sarah was a girl looking for sex, and Clive was looking, too. He even had an area to do it. Of course, if we didn't have the confessions, I would say the condom would back us up with Clive's DNA. Jona has still got to come through with that one.

'Peppa has a delusional feeling about men, the fact they like her all the time, whereas many don't. Seoras got to the house and saw the boots she was wearing. They'll convict her because that's a match. She followed Clive after he left and she killed him elsewhere. We're going through her car at the moment.

'She wasn't like Lorraine. She wasn't that clever. Then she

hanged him in a way that couldn't be suicide. She tried to pretend it was. Peppa isn't the cleverest person, but she was enraged when she'd seen her daughter having sex with Clive. She said that Clive, not Sarah, had betrayed her.'

'Then there was Esme,' said Macleod. 'Esme knew what was going on. She understood Roy had someone.'

'That's right; she confessed working out the mum-to-be. She'd also noticed Roy's love of Fern, or at least the way he looked at her. She put two and two together, found out Fern was pregnant, then she took matters into her own hands.'

'Poor Jenna,' said Ross. 'Lost her brother, and now her parents are both going to go down. They'll be locked up.'

'Poor Donald. Esme pulled him in,' said Hope. 'He's a mess down there.'

'What about Fern?' asked Davidson.

'The hospital said that Fern's going to be all right; the baby should carry on to full term. She's got her sister, at least, with her.'

'Right mess though,' said Macleod. 'A right mess that Hope's picked through and solved. Well done,' he said.

'I would suggest a little celebration,' said Hope, 'but it's three in the morning and you all need to get to bed. We'll come in tomorrow about ten and we'll start going through everything, wrap it up, and this weekend, we'll have a proper party. So, thank you, all. Now get off home.'

There was a general laughter in the room and everyone stood up. Hope slipped down off the desk, walked over to Perry. She waited while others left the room, and then she shook his hand.

'I know why Seoras put you on the team,' she said. 'You've got a mind for it. Your conjecture, your ideas, you were right on it. You read people in a way that I don't. He's right. I need you on the team, but you need to buckle up your ideas, too. That's maybe why he put you here. I won't take the rubbish. I won't take comments like you make at times. You could deal with being a bit more like Ross with his professionalism and he might do with seeing things the way you do.

'I was wrong about you, Perry, so welcome on board. If you want to stay, you can stay, but I won't take any sexist talk. I need you to be professional. It's not like when you were working with Macleod in Glasgow.'

'Okay,' said Perry. 'Thank you. A lot of people don't make an admission. They don't tell me when I get it right, and you're the boss, so we play it the way you want to play it. I'll see you in the morning. Thanks, Hope.'

He went to turn away, but he leaned back slightly, his jacket swinging to one side. He gave her a wink of his eye. 'I love a strong woman, though.' With that, he was gone.

'Well done,' said Macleod from across the room as Perry closed the door, leaving the two of them there. 'He's a work in progress, but he's clever. Darn clever. He impresses me with the way he reads people.'

'That's high praise indeed. He's slovenly, though, isn't he?'

'Very,' said Macleod. 'That bugged me when I worked with him, and the cigarettes, too. He was drinking more back then. He's cut down on that.'

'I wonder they didn't kick him out.'

'He was reprimanded. The last two units he's worked with wanted rid of him. In fact, they were about to get rid of him up here. I kind of saved him because you'll knock him into shape, and he'll be fantastic. Well done, Inspector. This one is yours, completely yours. You're not in my shadow anymore.'

Hope smiled; then she saw a face outside in the office.

'Looks like my ride's here,' she said to Macleod. 'Do you mind? I'm sure Jane would like you home as well.'

'She has already rung, told me the case was solved, and to stop playing. I'll see you tomorrow,' he said. 'You're organising the party for the team, not me; your team, although I expect an invite.'

'Always,' she said. She put her hand out and Macleod shook it. 'I hope I always do you proud,' she said.

'Why is that going to change? You saved a mother and a child today; well done—focus on that.'

Macleod turned to see the door of Hope's office opening and her partner, John, coming in. He gave the man a nod and walked out.

'Are you ready?' asked John.

'Darn right, I am.'

'You're in your spare clothes,' he said.

'I ended up jumping into a fire to save a girl. I didn't get burnt bad at all. She did, but she's going to be okay.'

'Do you want to talk about it?'

'No,' said Hope. She pulled John close and kissed him hard. Hope stepped back, took his hand, and walked over to where her jacket was hanging. She let go of John momentarily to put it on, flicked off the lights in her office and locked the door behind her before walking down the stairs of the station with him.

'The girl was pregnant,' said Hope. 'It feels good to have saved the little one.'

'You must be exhausted,' said John. 'I'll get you home. You're going to have a good sleep, nice bath when you wake up in the morning.'

'No,' said Hope. 'When this all kicked off, we were about

to start into a new section of life. The adrenaline's pumping through me. You don't know the thrill of saving someone like that,' said Hope, 'but tonight, you're going to find out just how it excites me.'

John smiled. 'Oh, let's get you home,' he said.

She stopped, turned him sideways towards her. 'Who said anything about home? We're leaving the phones in the car and we're going somewhere excitable, somewhere memorable.'

His face was a picture, a little nervous, somewhat apprehensive, and another part of him was absolutely beaming.

'Make the time,' said Hope. 'This is the time.' With every step towards the rear door of the station, she wanted to run. She wanted to grab John's hand like they were running along a beach, pulling him along in excitement. But nodding at a few of the night shift, she simply walked hand in hand with her man out to his car.

They got inside, Hope letting John drive, and as he reversed the car out of the parking space, he put his hand over onto her thigh. 'So where? Where'd you want to go?'

'Just drive,' she said, 'but out of Inverness. We'll see what. Somewhere we'll fancy.'

The rain, which had stopped only a few hours before, suddenly pelted down again as the heavens opened. Hope looked at John. 'Perfect,' she laughed and reached round the back of her head to take off the tie that kept her hair in a ponytail.

Read on to discover the Patrick Smythe series!

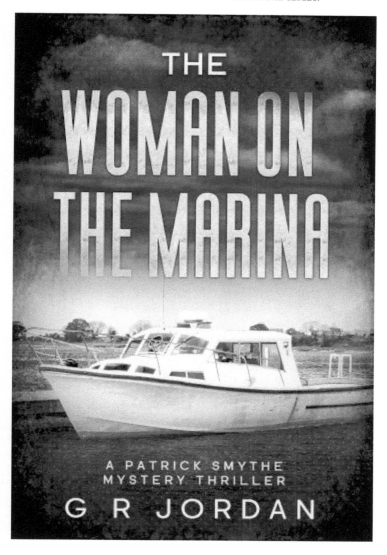

Patrick Smythe is a former Northern Irish policeman who after suffering an amputation after a bomb blast, takes to the sea between the west coast of Scotland and his homeland to ply his trade as a private investigator. Join Paddy as he tries to work to his own ethics while knowing how to bend the rules he once enforced. Working from his beloved motorboat 'Craigantlet', Paddy decides to rescue a drug mule in this short story from the pen of G R Jordan.

Join G R Jordan's monthly newsletter about forthcoming releases and special writings for his tribe of avid readers and then receive your free Patrick Smythe short story.

Go to https://bit.ly/PatrickSmythe for your Patrick Smythe journey to start!

About the Author

GR Jordan is a self-published author who finally decided at forty that in order to have an enjoyable lifestyle, his creative beast within would have to be unleashed. His books mirror that conflict in life where acts of decency contend with self-promotion, goodness stares in horror at evil, and kindness blindsides us when we at our worst. Corrupting our world with his parade of wondrous and horrific characters, he highlights everyday tensions with fresh eyes whilst taking his methodical, intelligent mainstays on a roller-coaster ride of dilemmas, all the while suffering the banter of their provocative sidekicks.

A graduate of Loughborough University where he masqueraded as a chemical engineer but ultimately played American football, Gary had worked at changing the shape of cereal flakes and pulled a pallet truck for a living. Watching vegetables freeze at -40'C was another career highlight and he was also one of the Scottish Highlands "blind" air traffic controllers.

These days he has graduated to answering a telephone to people in trouble before telephoning other people to sort it out.

Having flirted with most places in the UK, he is now based in the Isle of Lewis in Scotland where his free time is spent between raising a young family with his wife, writing, figuring out how to work a loom and caring for a small flock of chickens. Luckily, his writing is influenced by his varied work and life experience as the chickens have not been the poetical inspiration he had hoped for!

You can connect with me on:
🌐 https://grjordan.com
f https://facebook.com/carpetlessleprechaun

Subscribe to my newsletter:
✉ https://bit.ly/PatrickSmythe

Also by G R Jordan

G R Jordan writes across multiple genres including crime, dark and action adventure fantasy, feel good fantasy, mystery thriller and horror fantasy. Below is a selection of his work. Whilst all books are available across online stores, signed copies are available at his personal shop.

The Esoteric Tear (Highlands & Islands Detective Book 32)
https://grjordan.com/product/the-esoteric-tear
Precious gems are stolen from a museum tour of the Highlands. All but one of the gems are found dumped at the side of a loch. Can Clarissa Urquhart and her new team find the culprits before the gem finds a new home far from reach?

When the National Museum of Scotland has its gemstones stolen while on tour through the highlands and islands, D.I. Clarissa Urquhart faces the first test for her new section. On arrival at the scene, she is told that all but one of the precious items have been recovered, a relic with a history lost to the past. Urquhart must find its story, buried in secret societies, to understand who wants the gemstone before it vanishes from Scotland's shores.

Everyone's reality is different, but a precious stone will hold its price!

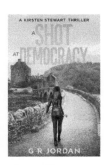

Kirsten Stewart Thrillers
https://grjordan.com/product/a-shot-at-democracy

Join Kirsten Stewart on a shadowy ride through the underbelly of the Highlands of Scotland where among the beauty and splendour of the majestic landscape lies corruption and intrigue to match any city. From murders to extortion, missing children to criminals operating above the law, the Highland former detective must learn a tougher edge to her work as she puts her own life on the line to protect those who cannot defend themselves.

Having left her beloved murder investigation team far behind, Kirsten has to battle personal tragedy and loss while adapting to a whole new way of executing her duties where your mistakes are your own. As Kirsten comes to terms with working with the new team, she often operates as the groups solo field agent, placing herself in danger and trouble to rescue those caught on the dark side of life. With action packed scenes and tense scenarios of murder and greed, the Kirsten Stewart thrillers will have you turning page after page to see your favourite Scottish lass home!

There's life after Macleod, but a whole new world of death!

Jac's Revenge (A Jack Moonshine Thriller #1)
https://grjordan.com/product/jacs-revenge
An unexpected hit makes Debbie a widow. The attention of her man's killer spawns a brutal yet classy alter ego. But how far can you play the game before it takes over your life?

All her life, Debbie Parlor lived in her man's shadow, knowing his work was never truly honest. She turned her head from news stories and rumours. But when he was disposed of for his smile to placate a rival crime lord, Jac Moonshine was born. And when Debbie is paid compensation for her loss like her car was written off, Jac decides that enough is enough.

Get on board with this tongue-in-cheek revenge thriller that will make you question how far you would go to avenge a loved one, and how much you would enjoy it!

A Giant Killing (Siobhan Duffy Mysteries #1)

https://grjordan.com/product/a-giant-killing

A body lies on the Giant's boot. Discord, as the master of secrets has been found. Can former spy Siobhan Duffy find the killer before they execute her former colleagues?

When retired operative Siobhan Duffy sees the killing of her former master in the paper, her unease sends her down a path of discovery and fear. Aided by her young housekeeper and scruff of a gardener, Siobhan begins a quest to discover the reason for her spy boss' death and unravels a can of worms today's masters would rather keep closed. But in a world of secrets, the difference between revenge and simple, if brutal, housekeeping becomes the hardest truth to know.

The past is a child who never leaves home!